THE MAN CALLED
BOWDRY

A HELLBOUND WESTERN

VAN HOLT

KING OF THE HELLBOUND WESTERNS

The Man Called Bowdry

978-1484019573

Cover and Book design: Three Knolls Publishing & Printing

First Printing, 2013. Printed in the United States of America.

CHAPTER 1

Not much is known for certain about the man called Bowdry. The bare facts are as follows. Sometime around 1880 he rode into Gray Buttes, Nevada—a long forgotten town—stayed for a time at the Pollard shack out in the hills and, after the old man was killed, made relentless war on the neighboring 3-Bar outfit which was run by the Wadley clan, known thieves and rustlers. Then he disappeared, to be seen no more, nor was he ever heard of again.

There were those who doubted if his real name was Bowdry. Some even suspected that he was really old man Pollard's long-lost son and that his name was Will Pollard, a mysterious gunfighter who roamed the early West. But before the stranger appeared it had never occurred to anyone that old man Pollard might have a son, and most would have laughed at the notion that he was related in any way to the legendary gunfighter who happened to have the same last name.

No one knew very much about the old man. No one even knew what his first name was. The people of Gray Buttes just called him old man Pollard or old Pollard, and smiled in a certain way when they mentioned him. He kept to himself, barely grunted if spoken to, and was considered rather odd or "funny."

There was nothing unusual about the old man's appearance. He was tall and gaunt, a little stooped from the years, his hair was white, and his eyes were faded blue. One day a few years before, he had come out of the desert looking used up. He had moved into an abandoned shack in the barren rocky hills south of town, on the edge of the range used by the 3-Bar, then owned and run by Harris Thacker. Thacker, seeing that the old man wished to be left alone, had told his hands to stay away from the shack and leave the old hermit in peace. Then the Wadleys had taken over the 3-Bar, after either buying Thacker out or scaring him away. He had left the country in a hurry before anyone could find out for certain which it was. Even his hands did not seem to know, but as for themselves, they were told to drift, and they drifted.

Then the Wadleys paid old man Pollard a visit, riding rudely up to his door and offering him a hundred dollars for the shack and waterhole, even though they said they knew he was just squatting on land he had no right to. The old man said he was there and meant to stay. Rufe Wadley, the red-faced, bullnecked leader of the bunch, advised him to think it over, but not take too long.

A few nights later, someone fired at the shack with a rifle, and some of the Wadley bunch were heard joking among themselves about it in the Waterhole saloon. Old man Pollard said nothing about it, but the next time he came to town for supplies, he brought along a double barrel shotgun and there was an old Civil War pistol stuck in his belt, a percussion Colt that had been converted to use cartridges. Two of the Wadleys were in town that day and they chuckled when they saw the old man, but said nothing until he left with his sack of supplies tied on behind the saddle, heading back for his shack.

Bowdry rode into town on a windy fall day when the buttes to the east were obscured by blowing dust. He rode in slowly on a dark horse, noticed by only a few people hurrying to get in off the cold windy street. When they saw him, they stopped for a closer look. He was wearing a long dark coat and a black hat pulled down over his eyes to keep out the dust.

He was not much over thirty but his copper-tinged dark hair was already touched with gray at the temples, giving him a dignified look. He was tall, a little over six feet, and straight without being stiff. It came natural.

His weathered brown face did not change as he rode down the street past the watching people. He glanced at them briefly with a remote smile in his blue eyes, but rode on to the livery stable without speaking to anyone.

In that empty land, the wind seemed always to blow. It was still blowing an hour later when Bowdry left the Nevada House, clean-shaven and wearing a corduroy coat and dark trousers. He was seen crossing the street to the Waterhole saloon. And it must have been there, sipping his beer and listening to the idle talk, that he first heard about the trouble old man Pollard was having with the Wadley clan.

While Bowdry was in the saloon, the hotel clerk, a dapper young man with large glassy gray eyes, went silently up the stairs to the stranger's room and let himself in. He glanced at the long dark coat hanging in the corner, then his eyes went to the saddlebags and blanket roll on the floor. It was in the saddlebags that he found what he was looking for: a worn cartridge belt with a walnut-butted Smith & Wesson .44 Russian in the holster. The empty cross draw holster on the left explained the slight bulge he had noticed under Bowdry's coat—if Bowdry was really the man's name. The clerk had heard that Will Pollard, the gunfighter, had a pair of Smith & Wessons, a Third Model Russian and a New Model American, and carried one of them in a cross draw holster.

When Bowdry returned to the hotel, the clerk was seated at the desk, reading a dime novel, his face like a mask. He looked at Bowdry through the blank windows of his eyes. Bowdry seemed lost in thought and scarcely noticed him. Taking his key, he silently climbed the stairs to his room.

When he came back down a short time later, carrying his saddlebags and blanket roll, he was frowning slightly. He had discovered evidence of the clerk's snooping. Something had not been put back just right.

The clerk, casually polite, pretended not to notice the chill in Bowdry's blue eyes. He laid his book aside and expressed surprise and regret that Bowdry was leaving so soon.

"I may be back in a day or two," Bowdry said, turning his back on the clerk. He had paid for his room in advance.

As Bowdry was leaving the hotel, two men rode slowly into town from the south—two men Bowdry would soon kill, Hunk Wadley and Grat Bowers. But he did not know that then, and they would not have believed it if someone had told them. They would have sneered at the thought. In fact, they sneered a little when they saw Bowdry glance their way and then turn down the street toward the stable. He did not look like much to them.

"Some dude," Bowers muttered, with a lopsided grin.

"Musta seen us comin'," the hoglike Hunk Wadley remarked, his red face and mean little eyes shining in a smile. "Looks like he's leavin' town. Old man Pollard should be so smart and git outta the country."

Bowdry got his horse from the stable, rode west until he was a half mile from town, then turned south. He had not asked anyone how to get to the Pollard shack, but he headed in that direction as if he knew the way, and walked his tired horse into the yard as the sun was dying behind the barren eroded hills to the west.

Old man Pollard stood in the door in the crimson afterglow with his shotgun cradled in his arms, looking up at the young man on the brown horse. It was faded, icy blue eyes meeting eyes that were a deeper, darker blue.

The stranger hooked a thumb back at the board sign behind him that said, "Keep the Hell off my Land."

"That's a pretty rude sign, considering this ain't your land. Not by rights."

"I got rights," the old man said. "Squatter's rights."

"Squatters ain't got no rights."

The old man patted the Greener. "This says I got rights."

The younger man glanced at the shotgun, then eased his position in the saddle. "Hear you're having some trouble," he said idly.

"Nothin' I can't handle," old Pollard informed him, not softening a bit.

Bowdry studied him silently and intently for a time, his eyes even more direct and probing than before.

At last it was the old man who looked away. He moved his shoulders in what might have been a shrug. "I don't need no gunfighter," he said.

Something like sadness appeared briefly in Bowdry's deep blue eyes, then vanished. His tone was matter-of-fact. "From what I hear, a gunfighter is just what you do need."

The old man's eyes were suddenly bitter and accusing. "How did you find me?"

Bowdry shrugged. "Just an accident. Back in town I heard about an old fool trying to get himself killed over a worthless shack that don't even belong to him. It sounded like you. Thought I'd ride out and take a look."

"You've had your look," old Pollard said harshly. "Now you can keep ridin'. Or go back to town and join the crowd that's laughin' and tellin' jokes about me, for all I care."

Bowdry seemed to sigh without actually doing so, and a sudden look of weariness aged his face. "I didn't see any crowd," he said. "Pretty dead place."

"That it is," the old man agreed. "No future around here for a young feller like yourself. You best keep ridin' before somebody gets the idea I sent for you or somethin'. I wouldn't want anyone to think that."

"I was sort of hoping you'd invite me to stay a few days," Bowdry said idly, his eyes taking in the weathered gray shack, the roan horse in the pole corral, and the steep rocky slopes that rose all around the place. "My horse could use a rest," he added. "So could I."

"I don't want you here, boy," old Pollard said hoarsely, his thin mouth oddly twisted. "I can't make it much plainer than that. You never had much use for me and I can't blame you for that. Was a time when I sort of hoped to see you again before I died. But it's too late for that now. Just ride on out of here and forget you ever saw me."

Bowdry appeared to swallow, though his face was like stone. He sat his saddle motionless and silent for a time, his cold blue eyes glaring at the old man. Then without a word, he stepped down and began stripping the gear from his horse.

"Are you crazy?" the old man cried. "This old shack ain't even worth me dyin' for, much less both of us!"

CHAPTER 2

It was almost dark in the shack. Bowdry sat on a bench against the wall, silently cleaning his guns—gleaming blue-steel pistols, one with smooth walnut handles and one with checkered walnut grips. Both fired the .44 Russian cartridge, which could be reloaded. Once he glanced at the Greener on pegs over the stove fireplace. He seemed unaware of the white-haired old man who sat at the end of the plank table, drinking bitter black coffee and staring at him with something like hatred in the icy blue eyes.

"I reckon you never heard what I said," the old man finally snarled.

Bowdry kept working on his guns as if he had not heard. But after a silence that grated on the old man's nerves and temper, he said in a soft, casual tone, "I'm staying. There's no point in discussing it."

"Just a waste of time," old Pollard said. "I was about ready to pack up and pull out. I was thinking of leavin' tonight."

Bowdry raised his blue eyes and studied the old man thoughtfully. "I think that's a good idea," he said. "You'll just get in the way here."

"*I'll* just get in the way?" the old man echoed, trembling with anger. "Who do you think you're talkin' to? I live here! This is my house! I never asked you to come here! You're the one who'll get in the way!"

The angry words had no effect on Bowdry. He reloaded the pistol with the checkered grips and slipped it into the cross draw holster, with the butt forward and to the right. Then he went to work on the Russian. The heavy gun looked light in hands that worked with the unhurried ease of long familiarity with weapons.

"This is the sort of thing I'm good at," he said. He meant fighting. "It's about all I know how to do."

"Oh, I've heard about you all right," the old man said maliciously, almost gloating. "I reckon everyone's heard about you, even the Wadley bunch. When they find out you're here I reckon they'll pack up and pull out as fast as they can."

Again, Bowdry did not respond right off. His hard impassive face did not change. What he felt, if anything, would remain trapped inside him until the day he died. Perhaps he did not want the old man to know he cared, if he did. When he spoke, his voice was quiet and casual, as before. He might have been discussing the weather. "They don't know me from Adam. If they find out who I am, it will be without any help from me."

"I see," old Pollard said, bitterly smiling and nodding his white head as if he had suspected as much all along. "I reckon I can't blame you for not usin' your own name. What name are you usin', if you don't mind me askin'?"

"Bowdry."

"Bowdry," Pollard said slowly, getting the feel of it. "Well, it ain't much of a name, but if you like it, I guess that's what counts. That what you want me to call you?"

"Suit yourself." Then, to the old man's surprise, Bowdry's lips twisted in a cold smile. "You can go on calling me 'boy' for all I care. I've reached the age now where it don't bother me."

Pollard watched him uncertainly in the fading light. When the old man spoke again his voice, though strong and steady, nevertheless sounded as if it might break. "When your ma died, I don't reckon anyone could blame you for pullin' out. She was the only reason you stayed around there as long as you did. You knew I'd soon be pullin' out again. Never was around there much. Can't blame you for feelin' the way you do."

"You talk too much," Bowdry said quietly.

The old man pulled the back of a gnarled hand across his tight, unpleasant mouth. "Yeah, I reckon I do. I always talked too much as far as you was concerned. Well, I'll say a little more while I'm at it. You might as well hear the rest of it, whether you want to or not. With both of you gone I couldn't stay there by myself, so I sold the old place for what I could get for it and decided I might as well catch up on my travelin', see all the things I missed. Well, I traveled. I kept travelin' for over ten years almost without stoppin'. Then one day I realized I was sick of travelin'. I never wanted to take another step or ride another mile as long as I lived. That's when I found this old shack. Hadn't been nobody livin' here for years. So I moved in and told myself I'd stay here for the rest of my days. I ain't regretted my decision either. I reckon I got my fill of travelin' for good. Just the thought of havin' to leave here, at my age, makes me want to set down and cry. I think I'd rather stay here and shoot it out with the Wadleys and their men. They ain't got no right to come in here and tell me I got to move out. They don't own this land. But I'd rather hit the trail again tonight than for you to get mixed up in this. I never was able to do much for you, but I tried not to do anything agin' you. From the things I kept hearin' about you, I figgered you would of got yourself killed a long time ago. But when it happens I don't want it to be because of me. I just ain't worth it, as you damn well know."

"I'm not doing it for you," Bowdry said. "I'm doing it because I don't know how to do anything else."

The old man's eyes were damp. But after a moment he shook his head. "I don't believe that. You were always good at anything you tried to do. Maybe you've convinced yourself that you became a gunfighter because you couldn't of been anything else, but you'll never convince me. You could of been anything you wanted to be. You just didn't want it bad enough. Like me."

"Maybe you're right," Bowdry said, after thinking about if for a moment. "Well, I guess it don't matter now. I'm what I am and you're what you are. I guess we'll have to let it go at that."

He did not appear to notice that the old man seemed quite pleased with himself, as if he had scored a small victory. Bowdry stood up and buckled on his gunbelt, then bent to tie down the holsters. He stepped over to the window and stood looking out toward the corral.

"Who's been coming to see you?" he asked.

The old man grunted in surprise. "You don't miss much."

"I know you didn't bake that light bread," Bowdry told him. "You're an even worse cook than me. Somebody brought it to you. Probably some old hag you've taken up with."

"Boy, it ain't like that," the old man muttered. "You don't know what you're talkin' about."

Bowdry shrugged. "It's none of my business," he said. "I think I'll go for a ride."

"I thought your horse was tired."

"I'm not going far."

"If you're smart you'll keep ridin'."

"If I was smart I never would've come here."

"Hell, I know that, boy."

Bowdry had been gone for nearly two hours—it seemed longer. Old man Pollard paced the shack floor, often going to the window to look out. And as he paced he muttered to himself, as he had got in the habit of doing, living alone.

"Said he wouldn't be gone long. Went off to town, like as not. May not even come back."

The old man's eyes grew damp and his mouth quivered. He would end up dying here all alone after all. No need to expect anything from that remote, hard-faced man who now called himself Bowdry. Whatever feeling had been between them once was long dead. Too much time had passed since they had seen each other, too many things had happened, and they had never been close to begin with. Now Bowdry had come here like a stranger, with cold empty eyes, talking about staying but perhaps never intending to do so.

"He'll likely take my advice and keep goin'," the old man thought aloud. Lately it seemed that he could not think unless he said the words out loud, and this made him wonder if his mind was going. His nerves were already shot. The last few days had about finished them. The waiting, the constant tension, the inability to sleep for fear they would sneak up on the shack, kick the door down and murder him. He had never had nerves like Bowdry, and he found it harder and harder to believe that the quiet, calm young man could be his son. In many ways Bowdry did not even seem human. Some of the usual emotions had been left out of him. It made the old man uneasy, for he had heard that many killers were like that. He used to be quite a reader of newspapers, and how often he had read about mankillers on trial for their lives, showing no expression throughout the proceeding. Of course, out here in the West, there usually was no trial. Often there was no law, which was the case here.

"He was always a strange, quiet boy and never let anyone know what he was thinkin'," old Pollard reflected. "But I sure never thought he'd turn out the way he has. A gunfighter!"

Just then a bullet shattered the only pane of glass left in the front window, and old Pollard, with a hoarse cry, grabbed his shotgun, though he knew they were out of range.

It was Hunk Wadley who had fired the lucky shot. He and Grat Bowers, on their way home from town, had stopped their horses on the boulder-strewn ridge top east of the Pollard cabin. Hunk Wadley drew his Henry from the scabbard and fired from the saddle, steadying his horse with his knees. When he heard the gratifying tinkle of glass, he chuckled in surprise, and Grat Bowers gaped at him in amazement. It was good shooting from the back of a horse, at night. Usually they wasted several rounds in the log wall before a well-placed shot found the window, which had been dark since that first night.

"That'll show the old bastard," Hunk said, laughing.

He levered the Henry to fire again, and at that instant his hat was jerked from his head. A gun exploded from the rocks thirty feet away, the orange muzzle flash almost as frightening as the sudden roar. Hunk Wadley's little pig eyes cut toward the flash, even as his rearing horse almost unseated him. He grabbed the horn with his left hand, bent low in the saddle, and spurred out of there, with Grat Bowers close behind him. The gun in the rocks blasted three more shots after them as they thundered down off the ridge and galloped south.

A short time later Bowdry trotted his horse down the slope and into the yard.

"Who's that?" old Pollard cried hoarsely through the broken window, his sweaty hands gripping the Greener. "That you, boy?"

Bowdry grunted an affirmative and turned his horse toward the corral. The old man came out with his shotgun, saying excitedly, "They was here again, boy! Shootin' at the house like before! Glass all over the place! You must of heard the shots! They ain't been gone but a few minutes!"

Bowdry stared at the old man in silence, then swung down from his horse and began unsaddling.

"I didn't know if you'd come back or not," Pollard said, moving closer. "Reckon I couldn't blame you if you hadn't. This is enough to get on anyone's nerves." He looked at the silent gunfighter. "Anyone who's got nerves, anyway."

Apparently the old man had decided he wanted Bowdry to stay. But it is doubtful if Bowdry had any illusions about the old man's change of heart. After a brief lapse, old Pollard was again thinking of himself first, as he always had when the going got tough.

CHAPTER 3

After a week nothing else had happened, and Bowdry and the old man were beginning to get on each other's nerves. Both loners, neither could endure another person's company for very long at a stretch, and neither was at ease around the other, though Bowdry suffered less discomfort and hid it better than the old man.

"You don't have to stay here and watch over me all the time, boy," the old man finally said. "I been lookin' out for myself for quite a spell now, and I was doin' okay before you showed up. Why don't you ride into town and let off a little steam, before you start gettin' cranky. I'd go myself, but it don't do me no good. I just get crankier. Never could stand to be around people. That's why I was gone so much when you was a boy. I wasn't off havin' me a good time, like your ma seemed to think. I was usually off by myself ridin' the back country, livin' off the land or maybe prospectin' a little."

"What about the Wadleys?" Bowdry asked.

"I got the Greener and the old Colt. If they come foolin' around here it will be at their own risk."

Bowdry stood at the shack door for a time, looking up at the rocks. The Wadleys might not come back any time soon, if at all, and he could not stay here and guard the old man forever. He had his own life to live, such as it was.

He shrugged. "My horse could use the exercise and I could use a drink. Anything I can bring you?"

"Can't think of nothin' I'm short of, and I swore off drinkin' a long time ago." The old man turned his pale cold eyes on Bowdry. "Never was as bad at it as some thought."

Bowdry did not say anything. After a moment he shrugged into his corduroy coat, carried his gear out to the corral and saddled the brown horse. When he was in the saddle, the old man appeared reluctantly at the door.

"I should be back before late," Bowdry said.

"Take your time," the old man grunted. "Just keep an eye peeled for them Wadleys."

"You do the same," Bowdry said.

He rode down to the waterhole, let the gelding drink, then followed the trail up over the east ridge, turning north toward Gray Buttes.

It was getting late and a cool wind stirred the stunted cedars on the barren rocky slopes. This part of Nevada was a lot like some parts of Arizona and Utah, but everything seemed grayer, bleaker, with fewer trees and more rocks. There were rocks and rock outcroppings everywhere. Some of the rocks had been worn into fantastic shapes by wind and rain and time, and the hills were stark and silent in the fading twilight.

When Bowdry was almost to the main road to town, which was also the 3-Bar Ranch road, he heard horses snorting and trotting along the road. He reined off the trail and watched them pass by in the deepening dusk. There were three of them, two he had seen in town his first day—Hunk Wadley and Grat Bowers—and one he hadn't seen before, a tall rawboned man with a black patch over one eye and a short gray beard, though he did not look that old in the poor light. According to the old man, the one with the black eye patch was called Lon. The old man had described most of the 3-Bar men and named some of them.

Grat Bowers squinted at Hunk Wadley and his heavy lips rolled back from his teeth in a grin. "What if that old man's in town, or that stranger we seen up in them rocks the other day?"

"They ain't got the guts," the red-faced Hunk Wadley said. "Atter shootin' at us that night they won't dare leave the place till they just have to. Then they'll make shore we ain't in town 'fore they ride in atter supplies or anythin'. But I hope they are there. Things has been dull lately."

Grat Bowers guffawed at that, and they rode on out of sight. Bowdry stared after them with cold eyes. He remained where he was for a time after their racket faded in the distance, trying to decide what he should do now, return to the shack or follow them on to town.

Bowdry had never thought of himself as much of a hero. He certainly did not stack up as much against the ancient heroes he had read about as a boy. He had never seen or slain a dragon, or ridden a winged horse. He himself did not breathe fire or hurricanes. He could not draw lightning from the sky and direct it at an enemy. But he could draw a gun in a fraction of a second and blast a man into hell, and he would prove it if necessary.

His weathered brown face resembling the rocks around him, he drew and checked first one gun and then the other. Then he rode on toward town, darkness soon overtaking him.

Once when he was about a mile from town, his horse whickered nervously and raised its head, looking toward some trees and brush to the right of the trail. With his left hand on the reins Bowdry held the horse to the same slow trot. His right hand went to the butt of the Russian Model and rested there as he rode on, expecting a shot, ready to draw and return the fire.

But nothing happened. He decided it was not the 3-Bar men. He had traveled slowly on purpose so as not to overtake them. It was probably some cautious traveler who had heard Bowdry's horse and pulled off the road, or a local cowhand who was not taking any chances, conditions being what they were. Bowdry did not much blame him, but it worried him that the other fellow had heard him first. That did not happen very often, and he did not intend to let it become a habit.

When he rode into town the street was dark and deserted except for three horses tied before the Waterhole saloon. Bowdry knew they would be the same three he had seen earlier.

He reined his own horse toward the Nevada House, where he had stayed for about an hour the day he rode into town, after paying for his room in advance. They should give him a refund, he thought, but he did not intend to mention it and he knew they wouldn't.

Stepping down, he wrapped the reins around the rail, glanced toward the saloon with cold eyes and then entered the hotel lobby. The fish-eyed clerk was not at the desk, nor was anyone else. Bowdry turned through another door into the dining room and ate alone at a corner table, covertly watched by a few silent townsmen who looked away when he glanced at them.

Bowdry found himself thinking about the old man out at the shack. He could not help feeling sorry for the old man, although it was not easy to feel sorry for someone who went out of his way to be disagreeable. He sort of wished the old man were here with him, enjoying a halfway decent meal. At least it was a change from their unvaried fare of bacon and beans, beans and bacon, and of course, cup after cup of bitter black coffee, strong enough to float nails.

Bowdry suspected that the old man, in spite of his brave talk, was afraid to leave the shack because of the Wadleys.

At that moment Bowdry heard coarse laughter from the saloon, and his fork cut through the tough steak like a razor.

He finished his meal, left some change on the table and went back out through the deserted lobby, idly wondering where the dapper clerk was. He paused on the veranda, looking toward the saloon.

Frowning slightly, Bowdry led his horse across the dusty street and tied him again next to the 3-Bar horses.

Hunk Wadley, Grat Bowers, and the one-eyed Lon were standing about halfway down the bar when Bowdry came in slowly through the swing doors. They fell silent and their grins became strained. Bowdry looked at them deliberately as he stepped up to the bar, but after that he did not look at them again and they did not look at him. There was no one else in the saloon except the sleepy bartender.

Bowdry quietly ordered a beer and sipped it in frowning silence, his mind on the three men down the bar. Once Grat Bowers whispered something and Hunk Wadley snorted. Bowers laughed uncomfortably and then coughed. Lon stood stiff and silent, keeping his one eye on his empty glass.

Bowdry rather enjoyed their discomfort. He started to order another beer just to prolong it, and to show them he was in no hurry. But he was uneasy about the old man at the shack, and also he had a feeling that if these three men left town ahead of him, they might decide to wait for him behind some rocks. They knew that if a stranger was killed in a night ambush, nothing would ever be done about it, and then they would have old man Pollard at their mercy.

Paying for his beer, Bowdry went out to the rail and untied his horse. As he was stepping into the saddle he heard Hunk Wadley say in the saloon, "I knowed he wouldn't stay long. He's scared, just like I figgered."

Bowdry started to get back down off his horse, but he did not want it to appear that he was looking for trouble. He knew that the best thing to do would be to pretend that he had not heard the fat man. After a moment he reined his horse away from the saloon and rode slowly out of town, his face set like stone.

He had gone no more than a half mile when he heard them coming at a gallop. He turned the brown horse around and waited at the edge of the road, his hand near his gun. If it was a fight they wanted he was ready to oblige.

They did not see him in the dark until they were almost to him. They had not expected to overtake him so soon, thinking he would waste no time getting back to the Pollard shack. They were not prepared to make a fight here, but they thundered straight toward him, evidently intending to crowd him off the road.

Bowdry stayed where he was and his right hand slid up the smooth holster toward the butt of the Russian. There may have been enough light for them to see this, for at the last moment they moved over and rode past him without slowing their reckless pace.

"Hell's wrong with you?" Hunk Wadley asked as they went by.

Bowdry turned his horse and sat there in the saddle looking after them until they were out of sight in the darkness ahead. Then he followed along cautiously in the wake of their settling dust, keeping the brown horse to a slow trot.

When he saw a good place to leave the road he turned off along a narrow valley with a ridge of eroded hills between it and the trail. The hills soon gave way to buttes looming above him and the valley became a rocky canyon curving away toward the southwest. He kept going, hoping to find a place not far ahead where he could climb out of the canyon without too much risk or difficulty. He did not want to turn back.

By now the moon must have risen, but down here at the bottom of the canyon it was pitch dark and slow going, for he had to pick his way through boulders and loose shale that had slid down from above. Once he thought he heard another horse walking on rock off to his left and he halted instantly to listen. But there was no more sound and he decided it must have been the racket of his own horse coming back off the canyon wall.

He moved on at a slow walk, passing a jumble of rocks where some stunted brush grew. Suddenly, for no apparent reason, there was a strange ringing in his ears and a cold chill went down his spine. He was not easily frightened, but at that moment he was afraid, and he had no idea what he was afraid of.

Then he remembered the sound he thought he had heard a few moments before, the sound of a horse walking along on the rocky ground. He knew now he had been right, but for some reason he felt certain it was not any of the Wadley bunch. This silent unseen man, whoever he was, belonged to an entirely different breed. There was an atmosphere of danger about him so real that Bowdry could feel it as he walked his horse carefully on past the jumble of rocks where he believed the man was hidden. He had no doubt that the man was watching him over the barrel of a gun and would use the gun if Bowdry made a sudden or suspicious move. Perhaps it was some outlaw on the dodge who could not afford to take any chances with strangers.

The brown horse snorted nervously, the last thing Bowdry wanted just then.

"We'll get out of here yet, horse," he said quietly to sooth the gelding. But he was really talking for the benefit of the man hidden in the rocks, letting him know he had no reason to worry. Bowdry was not a lawman or bounty hunter on his trail. Just a fellow minding his own business, and hoping others would to the same.

The brown horse shook his head, not liking the smell of the strange hidden man, and walked on down the canyon, with Bowdry sitting stiff in the saddle, braced for a bullet in the back. The shot did not come, but he did not breathe again until there were several huge boulders and a bend in the canyon between him and whoever that was back there.

At the first opportunity Bowdry put the horse up the wall of the canyon. The gelding had to scramble for it near the break in the rim and Bowdry heard rocks falling far below him. He was a little shaken by the time they reached the top. It was turning out to be a bad night all around. The trip to town had been a mistake. He had only gone to please the old man.

He halted on the boulder-strewn rim and looked about to get his bearings. Off across the hills there was a big orange moon, unnaturally bright, and not where Bowdry had expected it to be. Apparently he had not kept track of all the turns in the winding canyon. As a result he was not sure about his own location or the direction to the Pollard shack. He decided that his best bet would be to bear back toward the trail and not waste any more time, for now he was more concerned about the old man's safety than his own. Hunk Wadley and his pals might decide this would be a good time to pay the old man a visit.

He lined out across the rough, rocky hills, riding at a lope and even a gallop over terrain where he normally would have ridden at a walk or trot to spare his horse. But even at that reckless pace he had a growing conviction that he would be too late. He could not make up the time he had lost in the canyon, and the 3-Bar men had been traveling fast over a good road.

At last he reined in on the ridge with a sick feeling inside him, convinced that he was too late. In the bowl below him the old shack was dark and silent, and the door stood open, creaking in the cold wind.

Bowdry left his horse in the rocks, drew the New Model American from the cross-draw holster and crept down to the shack on foot. He stood with his back to the wall near the shot-out window, watching the rocks as he asked, quietly, "You all right, old man?"

There was no answer, as he had expected. There was no one in the shack—on one who was alive, anyway.

He went around to the creaking door, looked inside, and saw the old man lying on the floor near his old Colt revolver.

CHAPTER 4

Bowdry dug the grave and buried the old man by moonlight, when it would be harder for a sniper to pick him off from the rocks.

When it got light enough he looked for sign. It was not hard to find. One man had ridden up to the shack and shot the old man when he opened the door. That, anyway, was how it looked to Bowdry.

But he was puzzled. Why had the old man opened the door for a 3-Bar man, knowing what the result was likely to be? And why had one of them left the others and ridden over by himself?

Bowdry saddled his horse, got the old man's shotgun, and followed the tracks up over the ridge, the Greener across the pommel.

There was an old trail of sorts that ran down the narrow valley just east of the ridge. The 3-Bar men used the trail a lot, and had used it last night. There were a lot of tracks, though they were faint on the hard ground, and it was difficult to distinguish the tracks of the killer's horse from the others.

Bowdry followed the trail south toward the 3-Bar Ranch. He was gone for three hours and when he returned he knew as little as when he had started out.

On the crest of the east ridge he suddenly halted, surprised to see smoke rising from the chimney of the shack and a pinto horse in the corral that did not belong there.

Bowdry walked the brown gelding down off the ridge top, picked his way down through the huge rocks, halted again halfway down to study the old shack with worried eyes. From higher up he had already scanned the area all around it.

In the west at that time it was not unusual to go in a man's house when he was gone, help yourself to his grub, and make yourself right to home. It was the custom of the range. But in times of trouble it could be an unhealthy practice.

Bowdry had not come to think of the old shack as his. He certainly had not come to think of it as his home. He was not the sort of man to think of any place as home, unless it was the one he had left and lost long ago. But he had no intention of letting the place fall into the hands of the Wadley outfit, and this meant, for the time being at least, he had to keep possession of the shack. So he was not too happy to find someone there acting like he owned the place.

The fact that there was only one horse in the corral that did not belong there indicated that there was only one person in the shack. But things were so often not as they appeared, and Bowdry had not lived as long as he had by taking anything for granted. He got down from the saddle with his shotgun, tied his horse to a stunted cedar back in the rocks, and settled down to watch and wait.

The shack was in a little valley enclosed on all sides by steep rocky slopes. Not far from Bowdry's position was the waterhole at the edge of the rocks, perhaps forty yards from the shack and on slightly lower ground.

Suddenly the door opened and a young woman with long red hair, wearing jeans and a man's shirt, left the shack with a wooden bucket and walked down toward the waterhole. She was tall and shapely and walked in long strides like a man—she had long legs for a woman. When she got closer, Bowdry saw that she had a sunburnt freckled face and very clear bright eyes that were sort of green hazel. She was a fine looking young woman, almost beautiful in a wild untamed way. It would not have surprised him to see a gunbelt strapped around her lean waist, but she seemed to be unarmed.

As she bent down to fill the bucket at the waterhole, her long red hair falling over her slender shoulders and deep breasts, the tight jeans hugging her rounded buttocks—a sight that stirred even

Bowdry—three men came out of the rocks nearby and crept toward her. They must have been there all the time, waiting for Bowdry to return. They now moved up behind the woman. Hunk Wadley and Grat Bowers were grinning from ear to ear. There was a look of tense excitement in the one-eyed Lon's weathered face. Lon licked his chapped lips and rubbed his mouth with an unsteady hand.

The young woman, rising with the filled bucket, turned and saw them. She showed no alarm, just a cold anger in her catlike eyes. "What are you three doing here?" she asked in a suspicious, even accusing tone.

"Why, honey, we was just gonna ask you the same thing," the red-faced Hunk Wadley said with a dirty grin, openly admiring her curves. "You must be that Reardon filly."

She dismissed this last with a slight gesture and said, "I thought I'd come over and clean up the place a little. It seemed like somebody should. I reckon that's the old man in that grave over there?"

Hunk Wadley and Grat Bowers grinned at each other and Hunk said, "Yeah, I reckon somebody musta shot him."

"Somebody," Lucy Reardon said, regarding the three with cold eyes. "I wonder who it was."

Hunk Wadley shrugged, still grinning his stupid grin. "I couldn't say. He had enemies. Didn't nobody like him much."

"I liked him."

"I shore don't know why. A old man like that. I heerd about you comin' over here to see him, bringin' him pies an' such, and me and the boys ain't even managed to get a good look at you till now. We rode over that way a-purpose to see you, but you musta hid when you seen us comin'."

"You better stay away from there if you know what's good for you," she told him. "Josh Larkin will fill you full of lead."

"Nah, he won't do nothin'," Hunk said, taking a step toward her. "You've wore his mav'rick brand long enough. It's time we put ourn on you."

While Hunk talked, the one-eyed Lon had edged around behind her. He now grabbed her arms, pinning them to her sides and causing her to drop the water bucket. She screamed and kicked at Hunk Wadley as he lunged toward her, doubling him over. Then Grat Bowers stepped in grinning and punched her in the face, just as he would have hit a man. She grunted and went limp, stunned but not unconscious. Grat kicked her feet out from under her and Lon lowered her to the ground, none too gently.

Hunk Wadley was still bent over holding his fat belly, trying to get his breath. "Leave me at her first," he said. "It was my idea, and I owe her for tryin' to bust my—"

Bowdry had come out of the rocks unseen. Suddenly he was there with the shotgun in his hands and a deadly look in his cold blue eyes. From ten feet away he emptied both barrels into Hunk Wadley's red face as Hunk reached for his gun. Then he shifted the scattergun to his left hand, drew a long-barreled pistol with his right and shot the one-eyed Lon in the head. Grat Bowers, his grin turning into a taut grimace, cried out and held out his left hand toward Bowdry as if to stop the next bullet with his open palm. At the same time he was reaching for his gun with his right hand. Bowdry shot him in the chest, and when Bowers still tried to bring up his gun, Bowdry stepped forward and shot him again, this time in the head.

Lucy Reardon sat up with a dazed look in her eyes. She looked in disbelief at Bowers and the other two—alive and violent one moment, dead and still the next. It had happened too quickly, too suddenly, for belief. Then she looked at Bowdry's bleak face.

"You must be Bowdry," she said.

He nodded shortly, reloading his pistol. Then he broke the shotgun open, extracted the empty shells and put in two new ones from his coat pocket. He snapped the gun shut and cradled it under his arm.

"You better get out of here," he said. "The others may be around somewhere."

"Well, if they are they'll sure be after you now."

Bowdry dipped his head. "Exactly."

Lucy Reardon got to her feet, brushing off her clothes. "Do you know who killed the old man?" she asked. "Was it them?" She indicated the still warm bodies.

Bowdry moved one shoulder. "Them, or some of the others. It don't really matter."

"It don't really matter?" she echoed in amazement. "Don't tell me you blasted them just because of me!"

"Not hardly," he said.

"Then you think it was them?"

"I think they needed killing," he said, and going over to the nearest body he bent down to remove the dead man's gun and cartridge belt. He disarmed the others as well and slung the gunbelts and holstered revolvers over his shoulder.

"Do you think you'll need those?" Lucy Reardon asked.

"I may not," he said. "But they sure won't need them anymore."

"That's true," she admitted. "I was just thinking you had quite a few guns already."

Bowdry did not answer. He had turned to watch a man on a beautiful Appaloosa descend the steep ridge at a reckless clip. The horse was a flash of colors, chestnut and white and darker spots. The man looked pretty flashy and colorful himself in a black and white cowhide vest and a white Stetson. He had straw-colored hair, bright blue eyes and a strong nose. His teeth seemed too large and too white but from the way he displayed them it was clear they were his pride and joy.

As he reined in before them, his mouth open to speak, the girl lashed at him with her tongue, sounding both angry and shaken, though she had seemed calm enough up to now. "Where the hell were you? They tried to rape me. If he hadn't showed up they would have."

The straw-haired fellow gaped at her in surprise, then shifted his bright gaze to the dead men. "Them bastards!" he muttered. "I never figgered they had the guts."

"Where were you?" she asked again. "I thought you were comin' back last night."

Josh Larkin shook his big handsome head. "Don't blame me, Lucy. Comin' over here was yore idea, not mine. I never liked the idea of you foolin' around over here any of the time."

"Oh, I know that," she retorted. "You thought I was sleeping with that poor old man. It wouldn't surprise me if you was the one who shot him."

"Now Lucy, that's a hell of a thing to say!"

"It wouldn't," she repeated.

"I hate to interrupt this cozy little chat," Bowdry said dryly, "but I'd sure appreciate it if you two would drop by some other time. I'm expecting company and I'd sort of like to get ready for them."

"If you're expectin' trouble count me in," Josh Larkin said eagerly, flashing his bright smile at Bowdry. "I thought them bastards was my friends, but after what they tried to do—"

"Oh, who are you trying to kid!" Lucy Reardon said angrily. "You ain't worried about what they tried to do to me. You just want to get in it for the excitement."

Larkin grinned at Bowdry. "Women just don't understand, do they?"

Bowdry did not return the grin. His face remained bleak and hard. "Sorry," he said. "I work alone."

"Who said anything about work. I thought we'd ride over there, shoot up the 3-Bar, stampede their stock, and have ourselves a little fun."

"*Fun!*" Lucy Reardon exclaimed. "They tried to rape me and you talk about fun!"

Larkin gave her a tired but tolerant look. "Lucy, honey, why don't you head on back to the ranch. I'll be along later."

"Don't bother!" she said, her face flaming. "Go on and have your *fun*. And when it's over don't come crawling back to the LR looking for a place to hole up."

She strode to the corral, caught her pinto, threw on the blanket and saddle while Bowdry and Larkin watched in silence, and in a matter of moments she swung easily into the saddle and climbed the west slope.

"She'll cool off after a while," Larkin said to Bowdry. "She always does."

Bowdry shrugged. It was not his affair.

"You better reconsider my offer," Larkin said, grinning at him. "You're outnumbered about ten to one, and I'm purty good with a gun. We'd make quite a team."

Bowdry shook his head, watching Lucy Reardon disappear over the west ridge on her pinto. "It's not your fight," he said. "Stay out of it.”

“Hell, I was hopin’ for a little excitement,” Larkin said unhappily. “Things has been dull around here lately.”

“I hadn’t noticed.”

Larkin glanced at the three dead men on the ground, and his big teeth flashed in another grin. “Yeah, I see what you mean. Hell, Bowdry—if that’s yore name—there’s enough of them for both of us. Why try and keep them all for yourself?”

Bowdry regarded the rustler with a long silent glance, and Larkin shifted uncomfortably in his saddle. “It ain’t like they don’t need killin’,” he said. “I figger I might as well git me a few of them while the season’s open. ‘Sides,” he added with a smaller grin, tugging at the brim of his soiled white hat, “them bastards is just a pack of horse thieves and rustlers, tryin’ to hog all the range and stock for theirselves.”

Bowdry’s teeth showed briefly in a cold smile. “I figure a man like you could stand a little competition.”

Larkin chuckled, but without much humor. “A little, hell,” he said. “The way them bastards is goin’ at it they’ll soon have ever’ critter in this country wearin’ their brand, includin’ the LR stock, which is partly mine. Rufe Wadley already told me I might as well throw in with them. It’s beginnin’ to look like he’s right. But he wants to run things his way and I’m used to bein’ my own boss.” He shrugged. “Maybe I shouldn’t be tellin’ you all this, but my hunch is you don’t give a damn how many cows and horses I steal, so long as I let yores alone.”

“It’s nothing to me,” Bowdry agreed. “But like I said before, I always work alone. If you want to go hunting Wadleys, you’ll have to do it on your own.”

Josh Larkin’s grin became a grimace. “Well, it was just a notion, Bowdry. I thought you might like a little help, since you’re alone. If you change yore mind, I won’t be hard to find.”

He smiled again, but not very pleasantly, and turned the beautiful Appaloosa to ride off after Lucy Reardon, his ivory-handled Colts flashing in the sunlight.

Bowdry glanced at the tracks left by the Appaloosa. Then he squatted on his heels to study the tracks more closely.

CHAPTER 5

The bodies of Hunk Wadley, Grat Bowers and the one-eyed Lon returned to the 3-Bar Ranch tied across their saddles, causing much excitement. Several members of the clan were silent with shock, others howled their rage.

With the exception of the dead Lon, everyone at the ranch was related in some way to the Wadleys. Grat Bowers had been a distant cousin, as was Pink Deeble, the near-albino. Gray-whiskered Bones Grogan was an uncle with a son called Moose. Moose had been gone for some time but, unknown to the rest, was even now on his way home from Mexico with a stolen horse herd and three Mexican bandits he had taken up with. Clete Anson, a man with pale hair and glittering green eyes, had married the only Wadley girl and remained with the outfit even after his wife ran off to Mexico with her cousin, the aforesaid Moose Grogan, who lost her in a card game to a Mexican gambler. Later on she parted company with the Mexican, made her way back across the border and worked in a brothel in Tucson. She was fat and ugly but women were scarce on the frontier, and men not too particular.

There was a funeral of sorts at the ranch for the dead, with Rufe Wadley in an unbuttoned or buttonless old suit he had long since outgrown, reading from the Book, shaking his fist in rage and vowing not to rest until the killer was hunted down and made to pay for "this day's work." Then, while a few men stayed behind to shovel dirt on the blanket-wrapped bodies, the rest of the outfit, with the possible exception of Rufe Wadley himself, rode to town to get drunk and brag about what they were going to do to Bowdry just as soon as they could find him. But going and coming they skirted well around the old Pollard shack. Bowdry may have watched them pass or seen their dust from one of the boulder-strewn ridge tops, but no lead was exchanged.

A few days later Moose Grogan and the three Mexicans arrived at the 3-Bar with the stolen horses. Everyone seemed glad to see Moose except for Clete Anson and he did not say anything, for he was afraid of the scowling black-bearded young giant. It is reported that when he heard the news, Moose fell into such a towering rage that even Rufe Wadley was a little frightened. Shoving things out of his way, clenching one big fist and waving a huge old Walker Colt in the other, Moose roared that he would tear out Bowdry's liver with his bare hands and demanded to know why the others had not already done something. When Bones Grogan attempted to calm his raging son, Moose turned on him. He told the tall graying old man he had better shut up unless he wanted the kind of licking Moose had been planning to give him ever since he could remember. Moose had not forgot the time Bones had peeled the hide off him with a horsewhip. Moose still had the scars to remind him, and he had just been waiting for some excuse to pay the old man back for it. In his unreasoning anger, Moose backed the wide-eyed old man into a corner and dared him to try something like that now.

While the rest of the Wadley outfit looked on, silent and scared, the three Mexicans squatted on their heels outside, smoking brown cigarettes and chuckling. For some unknown reason they seemed to like the big mean gringo, Señor Moose. Otherwise they would have slit his throat before this, for they were bad ones, the worst of a lawless breed. Perhaps that was why they liked Moose—he was even more vicious and violent than they were.

In the house, Rufe Wadley said in his deep strong voice, sounding calm enough, "Cool down, Moose. This is uncalled for. Bones didn't mean no harm."

"You shut up too!" Moose shouted. "If you ain't got the guts to go after that bastard, keep out of the way and let me take care of it. Me and them three greasers out there can get Bowdry without a bit of trouble."

For a moment Rufe Wadley looked like he might explode. But he said nothing more. In a way it was almost amusing to see Moose snorting and bellowing the way Rufe normally did and Rufe assuming an air of philosophical calm.

So it was that Moose Grogan, for the short time he still had to live, seemed to be running things at the 3-Bar.

The old Pollard shack was in a bad location for defense, surrounded as it was by broken rocky hills. There were only two small windows and one door, with one completely blind side. And the waterhole was a good forty yards away over open ground. It would be impossible for one man in the shack to stand off a prolonged siege, with enemies sniping at him from the ridge. So Bowdry spent less and less time in the shack and more up in the rocks.

Not far from the waterhole was a rock-walled enclosure, a sort of natural corral with only one small opening that could be easily and inconspicuously closed with brush. Here he took both horses, and carrying bucket after bucket of water from the spring, he filled a small natural tank atop one of the rocks, afterwards brushing out his tracks. His saddle he hid nearby. The guns taken from Hunk Wadley and the other two were distributed at strategic points along the ridge. The lethal Greener he always kept with him now.

He had it with him, high in the rocks, the day Moose Grogan and the three Mexicans came after him. He saw them far below him and still some distance off, picking their way along the boulder-strewn floor of a canyon that ended in several cuts that somewhat resembled crooked fingers thrust into the steep slope, with spurs of rock and brush between.

Down one of these cuts Bowdry went at a run, darting silently from rock to rock. He dropped into the canyon just as the Mexican in the lead rounded the first bend, his bright dark eyes peering up from beneath the wide curved brim of his sombrero at the rocks above. He saw Bowdry drop from nowhere and land lightly on his feet directly in front of him, with the sawed-off shotgun at waist level but not yet aimed. The Mexican instinctively whipped out a long-barreled pistol, and Bowdry raised the twin muzzles of the Greener, firing from the hip. The buckshot tore the Mexican from the saddle. He died far from home with a somber look in his dark eyes and his teeth bared in pain.

Bowdry ran for the nearest rock. The second Mexican rounded the bend at a gallop, firing as he came. Bowdry raised the shotgun to his shoulder and fired over the rock, and the second Mexican was blown off his horse.

The third Mexican was close behind, but he wheeled his horse suddenly, firing back at Bowdry.

Bowdry's right hand left the shotgun, whipped toward his hip, jerked back up with a Smith & Wesson pistol. The gun roared and the Mexican swayed in the saddle. He grabbed for the large wooden horn and spurred back down the canyon, just as Moose Grogan left his saddle and sought cover among the rocks that had tumbled down from the rim.

One can only wonder why bold brave Moose Grogan—a born leader—sent the three Mexicans on ahead up the canyon. Perhaps, despite his boasting, there was a streak of cowardice in him. Certainly there was a streak of caution and animal cunning, combined with human craftiness. He must have had a feeling that, despite their precautions, Bowdry might discover their approach and welcome them with lead, and in that case, Moose had not wanted to be up front where the greatest danger was. Let the Mexicans go first. They were expendable.

The wounded Mexican dived from his running horse near Moose, who was already roaring at him not to run off. The Mexican rolled for cover, then reloaded his gun, trying to ignore the red stain spreading on his shirt. Moose, raising his black-bearded face cautiously, threw a couple of shots at Bowdry's rock. Bowdry stayed down, reloading the shotgun, and the screaming lead did no harm.

"No good," the Mexican said, looking sadly down at his wound. "Bullet he no come out."

"Why didn't you plug him?" Moose cried hoarsely.

"I try, but he shoot better," the Mexican said. "Tough hombre. He don't miss."

"I wish I'd been up there where you was," Moose said.

"I wish it too," the Mexican said, and Moose threw him a black look.

Just then a handful of small rocks rained down on Moose, one clipping him smartly below the right eye. He let out a startled roar not unlike that of an angry bear. The Mexican stared at him in surprise, then the white teeth flashed in an unexpected smile.

As Moose glared up the canyon in baffled rage, several more small stones pelted him. He gave a hoarse cry, his face turned purple, and he trembled in his fury. "Two can play that game!" he shouted, and grabbing some of the rocks, he raised up to hurl them back at Bowdry.

Bowdry was expecting that, and he was ready. Exposing only his hat, lean brown face and right shoulder, he thrust a pistol out at arm's length and fired.

The bullet struck Moose Grogan in the right breast and spun him around. He crashed heavily to the ground and lay stunned for a moment, then he pushed himself up to his hands and knees and reached for his big Walker Colt, staring in disbelief at the blood dripping from his great hairy chest onto one of the rocks Bowdry had thrown. "The bastard," he muttered, and suddenly collapsed.

After a minute he rose again and crawled back toward the rock, taking cover behind it and fumbling with his heavy gun.

Then, according to what the Mexican said later, Moose grunted and again collapsed face down behind the rock. Someone, firing from the canyon rim, had put a bullet in the back of his head. It sounded like a pistol shot—if so it was good shooting.

Somehow, in spite of his serious wound and the grave risk of a bullet in the back, the Mexican managed to climb onto Moose's horse and ride away down the canyon. He rode slowly, because it was the only way he could stay in the saddle, every moment expecting the bullet that did not come, even though he felt certain at least two guns were trained on him.

He rode all the way to the 3-Bar at a plodding walk, was helped from the saddle by not very gentle hands, and watched by hard suspicious eyes as he told his story. His bloody wound was ignored. When Rufe Wadley learned that Moose was dead, he turned away without a word, apparently not very saddened by the news. A smile glittered in Clete Anson's green eyes. But old Bones Grogan was shocked and angered, unwilling to believe his son was dead or to accept the Mexican's version of what had happened.

"How do we know he's tellin' the truth?" Bones asked, glaring blackly at the Mexican's sweat-beaded face. "I never seen a greaser yet I'd trust. They're all born liars. How do we know *he* didn't shoot Moose in the back of the head, and just make up that story about it bein' somebody up on the canyon rim?"

"Why would he kill Moose?" Rufe Wadley asked, idling in the background.

"Maybe 'cause Moose wouldn't let the yaller dog run out on him. It's happened before, lots of times." Bones turned his bitter eyes back on the Mexican "You tryin' to say Bowdry just let you ride off without even tryin' to stop you?"

The Mexican nodded respectfully. "Si. That is what happened. Maybe he don't like to shoot in the back."

"I think he's lyin'," Bones insisted. "Tie him to that cottonwood and let me work on him a little. I'll get the truth out of him."

"A waste of time," Rufe Wadley said impatiently. "He'd die before he'd change his story. But I figger he's tellin' the truth anyway."

"Then who could have shot Moose, unless it was him or Bowdry?" old Bones cried. "You don't believe that story about it bein' somebody up on the rim, do you?"

Rufe Wadley shrugged. "Maybe Bowdry's got somebody helpin' him. If he has, we'll find out who it is before long." He looked at the Mexican. "You better go. I'm sorry about that hole in you, but there ain't much we can do for you, and it wouldn't be a good idea for you to hang around here."

"Si, señor," the Mexican said, looking at old Bones Grogan. "I think you are right."

Rufe Wadley nodded. "Couple you boys help him back on his horse."

"That's Moose's horse!" old Bones cried.

"Moose won't need it no more," Rufe Wadley said, going back into the house.

The Mexican took the long trail back to Sonora, stopping en route to get the bullet dug out of him, and to tell what had happened in the canyon.

CHAPTER 6

Up to now Bowdry had kept pretty close to the old shack, except for that one trip to town that had resulted in the old man's death. But he was tired of waiting in the rocks and he began to prowl the rugged, cedar-dotted hills out beyond the rocky ridges that encircled the shack, trying to get a clearer picture of the country roundabout. He took to slipping away, by one of the hidden trails through the rocks and brush, and staying gone for hours, sometimes for a whole day. Sometimes he went on horseback and sometimes on foot.

East of the rocky cedar slopes the hills were higher and covered with piñon and juniper, rising in wavy ridges toward a dark mass of pine-clad mountains in the distance. There was a little bleached grass in these foothills but for the most part the ground was barren and rocky except for the stunted trees.

One afternoon Bowdry, wearing moccasins and carrying the shotgun, was returning from one of his hikes when he came upon fresh horse tracks in the trees no more than half a mile from the shack. This was on the cedar slope just beyond the east ridge. A single horse had made the tracks, and they did not appear to be more than a few minutes old.

Bowdry bent down briefly to study the tracks, then his eyes followed the probable course of the horse and rider on down through the trees toward the foot of the slope. The trees were scattered, but outcroppings of rock and boulders obstructed his view beyond thirty paces.

Suddenly he heard a horse snort and the ring of an iron-shod hoof on rock—not where he had expected the horse to be. Then as he rose cautiously to his feet, he saw three riders plodding south through the stunted forest. They passed by off below without seeing him, and he could hear them talking.

"We gettin' a little close, ain't we, Gord?"

The man who answered bore an unmistakable resemblance to the late Hunk Wadley. No doubt a brother. A little younger perhaps, but just as stout and paunchy, with a jolly red face and bright squinty little eyes. "Nah," he said. "There ain't nothin' to worry about. He ain't got no rifle, and we out of range anyways."

"He's liable to come atter us though."

"Let him come," Gord Wadley said. Then his fat downy cheeks creased in a grin. "You scared, Pink?"

Pink Deeble had just missed being an albino. His sunburnt face looked pink—hence the nickname. "It ain't that, Gord. It's just that—"

As they passed near a big rock, a gun roared and Pink Deeble slumped over in the saddle, grabbing the horn with both hands to keep from falling.

"Git the hell outta here!" Gord Wadley cried, already spurring his horse away, with his scared round face peering back toward the rock.

The third man, who had not spoken, had pale hair and wild green eyes. He grabbed the reins of Pink Deeble's horse in passing and followed Gord Wadley on around the slope at a gallop, dodging through the low trees, bending under limbs that very nearly tore the dazed Pink Deeble from the saddle. But somehow Pink kept his precarious seat and they soon disappeared, heading south toward the 3-Bar.

Bowdry stepped behind a shrub and waited. Minutes later he caught glimpses of a horse and rider moving silently away through the trees at a walk. The horse was red, either a bay or a sorrel, and the skirt of a brown suit coat was pulled up above the bone handle of a Colt revolver. But Bowdry never got a clear look at the man's face. The man walked the horse on around the hillside and was soon gone.

Bowdry had made no move to stop him, even though he knew that he himself would be blamed for this. He was not the sort of man to appreciate that kind of assistance—yet he was more puzzled than angry. He wondered who the man was and why he had bought chips in this deadly game.

There was soon little doubt in anyone's mind as to what the Wadley outfit thought about the shooting. As soon as Gord Wadley and Clete Anson got the wounded Pink Deeble to the 3-Bar, Rufe Wadley sent Anson back to town after Doc Batter. Doc Batter was a small old man with a mouth full of rotten teeth. He was rarely sober, but drunk or sober he never stopped talking. Even when by himself he talked to people who were not there, and often argued with his long dead wife, sometimes meekly apologizing afterwards. But mostly he talked about the miracles he had performed on his patients and about the people who owed him money. "Ever'body wants doctorin' the minute they need it, but they put off payin' for it just as long as they can," he often said.

When he got back to town in his buggy, he had quite a story to tell about his "close call" out at the 3-Bar. In those days there were usually a few old-timers seated on the hotel veranda of an evening, to whittle and talk about the "old days," when they were young, and enlarge upon the latest gossip. When Doc Batter left his poor old horse and buggy in the street and joined them, they wanted to know if that Pink Deeble feller had cashed in his chips.

"Why, I saved that boy's life," the old doc informed them, helping himself to a chair and a drink from his flask. He ignored the wistful glances at the flask, returning it to the pocket of his shabby old coat. "Course, it wasn't no bad wound, bullet just plowed a little furrow acrost his chest, but he was all set to die before I got out there and told him he never had nothin' to worry about. You'd think they'd be grateful, but they never said a word about payin' me, and I knew better than to bring it up."

"What was this close call you mentioned, Doc?" someone asked.

"Why, it ain't safe to go out in them hills, boys. A feller could get hisself shot just for bein' out there, the way things is now. What if that Bowdry feller had seen me goin' to patch up someone he'd just gone to the trouble to shoot? Chances are he wouldn't like it a bit. He might even get the notion I was on their side or somethin'."

"Then there ain't no question it was Bowdry what done it?"

"Not in their minds there ain't. They was so mad that Gord Wadley took my shotgun to go after Bowdry with. He said he'd bring it back when they get Bowdry, but I prob'ly won't never see it again. It wasn't bad enough they never paid me nothin' for all the trouble I went to and riskin' my neck. They had to take my double barrel Ethan Allen that I kept to shoot birds and rabbits with. Took all my shells too."

"You mean they're goin' after Bowdry with birdshot? Against his buck?"

"I reckon. I doubt if they'll know the difference till it's too late. I don't think that Gord Wadley could even read what it said on the box. But the others will have their pistols. Never seen so many pistols. I didn't see more'n one or two rifles, though. A Henry I think and one of them old Colt revolvin' rifles."

"I seen that gun the other day when they was all in town, buyin' shells and talkin' war. Looked like a good old gun."

"I just hope they bring my shotgun back when they're done with it," Doc Batter said. "I can't afford to doctor them no more if they aim to keep my guns."

"You're lucky they let you leave, Doc. The next time they may keep you out there to look after their wounded. Or maybe put a bullet in you for your trouble."

"It wouldn't surprise me none," the old doc said, reaching for his flask. "I've had some close ones in my time. Did I ever tell you about the time Cactus Charlie made me doctor his pet rattlesnake? Biggest snake I ever saw. Cactus only kept it so's his mother-in-law wouldn't try to move in with them."

Just then Miles Hinton, the hotel desk clerk, came to the door and stood there idly, listening to the talk.

Doc Batter looked around at him. "You workin' today? I thought it was your day off."

"It is," Hinton said, distantly polite. "I was reading in the lobby. Couldn't help overhearing some of what you said. You say Pink Deeble wasn't hurt much?"

"No, he was a mighty lucky boy. Whoever it was shot at him from the side and must of led a little too much for the speed of the horses. He'll have a sore chest for about a week, but that's about all." Then the old doctor gave Hinton's blank face a closer look. "If you still ridin' out that way to shoot targets, you want to be careful. Somebody's liable to use *you* for a target."

Miles Hinton shrugged, then said, "I guess it could happen. I understand that sort of thing goes on quite a bit during a range war. Anybody's fair game who happens along. But you're probably in more danger than I am." He looked at the old doctor with his strange cold eyes. "What you said about Bowdry not liking for you to patch up somebody he's shot—you ought to keep that in mind."

CHAPTER 7

"Bowdry! Hey, Bowdry, where the hell are you?"

Josh Larkin sat his restive Appaloosa in the yard before the shack, scowling at everything in sight—or perhaps at something he could not see, since there was nothing in sight except the old log house, the empty corral, and the barren rocky slopes which he scanned with a cold glitter in his bloodshot eyes. The left eye was swollen almost shut, and his big teeth were bared in a look of pain. He looked like a man who had seen better days. His horse was dirty and flecked with foam, his gaudy clothes were soiled and torn, and his white-handled guns looked like cheap toys that someone had palmed off on him as the real thing.

Bowdry finally emerged from the rocks with the shotgun cradled in his arms, taking his own sweet time and seeming to derive some satisfaction from the growing irritation on Larkin's face.

Larkin tugged his hat down over his eyes and scowled at the silent gunfighter. "You seen anything of Lucy?" he asked.

Bowdry moved his head about an inch to one side, watching Larkin blankly. He seemed to be studying the half-shut eye which Larkin kept turned away from him, glaring at him with the other eye.

Larkin pulled his soiled white hat still lower, and his eyes seemed darker in the shadow of the brim as he once more swept the rocky slope with a sharp glance. "I figgered she rid over this way," he said. "She usually does when she gits mad. Or did anyway when the old man was alive. I thought when he was killed that would put a stop to it. But now I don't know. She's tuck off somewhere, and I can't even find her tracks."

Bowdry remained silent, deliberately watching Larkin's swollen left eye.

Larkin shifted uncomfortably in his saddle, frowned at him and said, "Me and her had a little argument. She gits me so mad I can't keep from slappin' her. But she don't slap back. She draws back her fist and lets me have it just like a man. I never saw a woman who could hit harder or one worse about fightin'. Then she either tries to run me off or takes off herself and I don't see her again for two or three days. Used to come over here and stay with that old man, just like she was his daughter. Or maybe his wife, I never did figger out which it was."

"Is that why you killed him?" Bowdry asked.

Josh Larkin's mouth fell open and he shot Bowdry a startled look. "Me?!" he exclaimed. "Hell, I never killed that old man! Don't tell me you believe what she said the other day!"

Bowdry studied the rustler's face carefully, his own a mask. "You were over here the night he was killed. Or your horse was."

Larkin's eyes—even the hurt one—widened in alarm. He jerked off his bandanna and mopped sweat from his face, though the day was not hot. "Yeah, I come over here," he said. "Lookin' for that crazy girl. But I never shot that old man. He was already dead."

Bowdry shifted the shotgun in his arms, and the twin muzzles moved a little more in Larkin's direction. "That might be hard to prove," he said.

Larkin again rubbed his face, this time with his bare hand, though he still held the bandanna in the other hand. "That's why I never said nothin' about it," he said. "I knowed nobody wouldn't believe me. Ever'body would think I killed him myself because I didn't like Lucy hangin' around over here so much."

After watching him in silence a moment, Bowdry nodded slightly. "Could be," he said. "But it's also possible that you killed him yourself, thinking the Wadleys would be blamed for it."

"No, that ain't possible neither!" Larkin said, his voice shaking a little. " 'Cause I never done it." Then his bloodshot eyes darted a quick glance at Bowdry. "If you think it was me, how come you still fightin' the Wadleys? Or are you?"

Bowdry moved his shoulders slightly. His weathered face was bleak and hard and at that moment he looked closer to forty than to thirty. "Whether they actually killed him or not ain't as important as it might seem. They wanted to kill him, they even tried to several times, and sooner or later they would have. If somebody else beat them to it, it don't lessen their guilt any, as far as I'm concerned." Then his blue eyes got a lot colder and bored into Josh Larkin. "But if somebody else did do it, thinking they'd be blamed, then that man needs killing just as much as they do. Maybe even more. At least they've never made much of a secret of their intentions or tried to put the blame on anyone else."

"I tell you I never killed that old man!" Josh Larkin cried, now red-faced and angry. "But the minute I seen him lyin' there I knowed I'd be the one blamed for it. Before them Wadleys showed up, I got blamed for ever' bad thing that happened around here, and it don't look like things has changed much."

"If it wasn't them or you," Bowdry said, "who could it have been?"

"How the hell do I know?" Larkin asked. "I just figgered it was some of that Wadley bunch."

"I ain't ruled them out," Bowdry said. "But one thing keeps bothering me. Before that night they always stayed up in the rocks and shot at the house with rifles. But he was shot at close range—with a handgun."

"Don't look at me," Larkin said. "I tell you it wasn't me."

"If it wasn't you or them," Bowdry said thoughtfully, "that leaves only two other people that it could be."

"Two others!" Larkin exclaimed. "I can't even think of one!"

"That makes it look bad for you then," Bowdry said. "Because I don't think it was the Wadleys."

"I find that hard to believe," Larkin said, suddenly calmer for some reason. "No matter what you say, I don't think you're the kind of man to blast the daylights out cf someone the way you done to Hunk Wadley and them other two, not without you had a good reason for it. You must of thought they were the ones killed the old man, at least at the time. You never thought it might have been me till after what Lucy said, did you?"

"That's when I noticed your horse's tracks," Bowdry admitted. "They were the same tracks somebody left here the night he was killed. But till then I just figured it was one of the Wadleys."

"Wait a minute," Larkin said. "You sayin' my horse was the only one that come here that night?"

Bowdry nodded, watching him. "If anyone else was here they did a good job of hiding their tracks. That's why I think it was the Wadleys. They ain't that careful or that good."

"But that don't make no sense!" Larkin said. "Somebody else had to be here. No matter how it looks to you, I know I never killed that old man!"

Bowdry's hard face did not soften. There was no hint of sympathy in his steady blue eyes. But after a moment he nodded his head slightly. "I halfway believe you," he said. "I don't know why. All the evidence points at you. You were here, you had the motive and the opportunity, and my guess is you could do something like that and never lose a wink of sleep over it. But somehow I don't think it was you."

"It wasn't," Larkin said, grinning with relief.

"I've been wrong before," Bowdry said. "Once or twice. Don't do anything to make me wonder if I'm wrong about you."

"I'll try not to," Larkin said, once again his old reckless, nonchalant self. He started to lift the reins, then said, "Wait a minute. I nearly forgot why I come. You never did actually say you hadn't seen Lucy. You only shook your head a mite. I'd rather hear you say it out loud."

"I ain't seen her," Bowdry said quietly.

Larkin nodded, but the cold glitter was back in his bloodshot eyes. "I'll take yore word for it, Bowdry," he said. "But that's my girl and I don't want her foolin' around over here. I got a hunch I could trust you with anything else I got, maybe even my life, but I wouldn't trust any man alive with my girl. I just wanted you to know that."

Bowdry nodded, his eyes turning cold again. "I got that impression," he said. "Maybe you can keep her away from here, now that the old man's dead. I hope so."

"I sure aim to try," Larkin told him, and turning the Appaloosa, the rustler rode back toward the LR Ranch.

Bowdry watched until the flashy horse and rider had disappeared over the west ridge. Then he turned and went back up through the rocks the way he had come down.

When he was halfway up the rough slope, he suddenly stopped, frowning at the red-haired young woman who stood beside a rock, smiling at him.

"If I was a Wadley you'd be dead," she told him.

"I was thinking of that," he said. "What are you doing here?"

"I came to see how you're getting along," she said.

"I was doing all right till you showed up," he said, and glanced about with cold eyes. "Where's your horse?"

"Back over the ridge a piece. I wanted to make sure Josh wasn't here before I rode in. I figgered he would be. He's always follerin' me around."

"Maybe he don't trust you."

She shrugged. "That's his hard luck. It ain't my fault if he thinks everybody else is like him. He's always puttin' his brand on other people's stock and I guess he thinks someone will try to put their brand on me."

"You better go," Bowdry said. "I've got enough trouble already. I don't need any more."

She raised both hands and smoothed back her long red hair, so that her breasts stood up and pressed against her hickory shirt. She was watching Bowdry with a smile in her bold eyes. "I thought you might need some chuck or something," she said. "How are you fixed for supplies?"

"Got everything I need."

"You sure now?"

She kept smiling and he kept frowning. He didn't say anything.

"You must not get much of a chance to cook anything decent to eat," she said. "I could bring you some stuff, like I done for the old man. Or cook while you keep watch."

"The old man's dead," he reminded her.

"You ain't blaming me for that, are you?"

Bowdry shrugged. "You said yourself it might have been Josh Larkin. If he shot the old man, it was because of you. And if he comes after me, it will be because of you."

"Ah, I just said that 'cause I was mad. He gets crazy jealous at times, but I don't much think he'd do something like that." After looking away for a moment, she met Bowdry's glance and smiled at him. "Anyway, me and him are about finished. I already told him to get his cows off my range. He said they were all his 'cause he stole them, and I told him to take them all then. That's what we had that argument about."

Bowdry scanned her freckled face. It was a little red, but that seemed to be sunburn and natural high color. "Looks like he got the worst of it."

Her white teeth flashed in a smile. "He usually does. I sock him a good one and then get out of his way till he cools down. I can outrun him on foot, and then I sneak off on my horse when he ain't looking. He always comes after me, but he's not much good at following tracks."

Bowdry shook his head. "When a man and a woman have a fight and the man comes out of it with a black eye—I don't know."

Lucy Reardon laughed, then said, "I was just paying him back for the one he give me the last time. He made out like it was a accident, but I think he was lying. He lies about nearly everything."

"A pretty good liar, is he?" Bowdry asked.

"About the best I ever saw. I believed everything he told me till I found out nearly everything he said was a lie. He's lied so much, even he don't always know when he's lying and when he ain't. He really believes most of what he says. I guess that's why he's such a good liar."

Bowdry thought that over in silence.

"Well, I got to go," Lucy Reardon said. "I'll be coming back to see if you're all right and if you need anything."

"I don't think that would be a good idea," Bowdry said.

Lucy Reardon looked at him, smiling a little. "I think you're just scared I'll get shot by mistake or something. But you don't have to worry about that. I can take care of myself."

"I don't doubt that."

CHAPTER 8

Gord Wadley grinned at his older brother. "What you doin' settin' there behind that desk? Old man Thacker wouldn't like it if he was to come back and see you makin' yoreself to home at his desk that way, goin' through his papers."

The chair creaked as Rufe Wadley shifted his ponderous bulk. He raised a plump hand and smoothed his long heavy sideburns and curling mustache. "Not much he could do. He signed ever'thing over to me."

Gord Wadley's grin widened. "It's just a piece of paper. You never paid him nothin'."

"The paper says I did. Anyway, he ain't the one I'm worried about."

"I know who you're worried about," Gord said, still grinning. "It's Bowdry."

A look of impatience crossed Rufe Wadley's bloated red face. "We should of left that old man alone. I figgered it would be just as easy to scare him off as it was Thacker. That old shack ain't worth nothin' much and it didn't even belong to him. I shore never figgered he'd send off for no gunfighter. Now it looks like Bowdry aims to keep the place himself. Whoever killed that old man sure played hell, and I can't even find out who done it."

"I don't think it was none of our outfit," Gord Wadley said, still looking jolly and pleased with the world. "You said just to keep tryin' to scare him off a while longer, and that's all we done. I figger Bowdry killed him and let on like it was us."

Gord Wadley studied his younger brother thoughtfully for a time, his fat hands clasped behind his bull neck. "You don't think it could have been Hunk and Grat and Lon, the night they went into town? They wouldn't of admitted it, even if it was them. Not after I said not to hurt him."

"I don't much think it was them," Gord said. "But I guess they could of done it and just not said nothin' about it."

"Well, it don't matter now," Rufe Wadley said with a weary sigh. "Bowdry killed them and we can't let him get away with it."

"We shore can't," Gord Wadley agreed. "We're all ready to go atter him. Just waitin' for you to give the word."

A look of irritation came into Rufe Wadley's reddish eyes. "I understand one of the new men won that shotgun from you in a card game. The one called Whitey, I believe."

"Yeah, he got lucky."

"Lucky, hell," Rufe Wadley growled. "Luck never had nothin' to do with it. You know you can't play poker worth a damn. And that shotgun wasn't even yores."

"Old Doc Batter won't say nothin'," Gord Wadley said complacently. "He knows better."

"Maybe not to us. But he'll say plenty to ever'body else. You never should of taken his shotgun. We can't run *him* out of the country. No tellin' when we may need him again, the way things is goin'."

"Bowdry won't shoot nobody else," Gord said. "Whitey and them says they wouldn't mind goin' atter him by theirselves, iff'n you don't want the rest of us to go. They talk like it won't be no trouble to git him."

Rufe Wadley gaped up at his fat, grinning younger brother in amazement. "That's just the way Moose and them greasers talked. Look what happened to them."

For once Gord Wadley had nothing to say. His grin became a little uncertain, his plump round face a little redder.

Rufe Wadley shook his head. "No, we can't go chargin' in there like Custer and get shot all to hell the way them others did. We got to have a plan."

"You been tryin' to think of one now for quite a spell," Gord Wadley said. "You ain't come up with nothin' yit."

Rufe Wadley's red eyes glowed like live coals. "I'm workin' on it," he said.

The four new men lounged on the top pole of the corral watching two of the hands work with a sleepy little dun horse that bucked like it had a cougar on its back every time someone got in the saddle.

The new men showed little interest in the dusty activity in the corral and no inclination to try to ride the horse themselves. Three of them were of a type, silent, shifty-eyed, scarred by forgotten battles with other men, bad animals, and the hard land itself. The fourth was a boy with stringy blond hair and a sneering bony face.

Now and then, one of them glanced over his shoulder at the low-roofed log house, or swept the rugged hills roundabout with a sharp glance.

Gil Darby—a small dark man with a black stubble along his jaws—spat a stream of tobacco juice, wiped his mouth with the back of his hand, and said, "This here ain't a bad layout. I mean, fur fellers like us."

The others did not bother to reply, gave no sign that they had heard. They had something else on their minds.

The kid, Rex Medlin, glanced at the house and said, "This is ridiculous. That big tub of guts is settin' there tryin' to think of some complicated battle plan that won't work when the time comes, when all it needs is one good man."

Whitey had a brown face like old leather and dirty white hair that fell to his collar. His pale eyes gleamed with cold amusement as he said, "One good man is right. Not no green kid."

The kid sulked in silence. He would not have taken that from anyone else, but he knew better than to tangle with Whitey.

Whitey suddenly dropped to the ground like a big cat and padded away on silent moccasins. Whitey had once scouted for the army in Arizona and had learned a lot from the Apache scouts.

"Where you goin', Whitey?" Gil asked.

"Think I'll try out that shotgun," Whitey said.

Without another word to anyone, Whitey saddled his horse and rode off with the shotgun across the pommel. That was the last time anyone saw him alive.

At least no one ever *admitted* seeing him alive after that. Someone saw him—the man who killed him.

But at this point, Whitey still had several hours to live and he had every intention of lasting a lot longer than that.

Beyond the first hill, he broke the shotgun open to make sure it was loaded. That was when he noticed that the shells were birdshot. His lips twisted in disgust. He was not hunting birds, or rabbits either. He checked the nearly full box in his saddlebag, but they were birdshot too. Well, birdshot would just have to do. At close range it would tear a man up pretty bad. And he had his single-action Colt if he needed it.

Shouldn't of sold my Sharps, he thought. But he had been broke and hungry at the time, and he could not eat a buffalo gun. Not that he had ever hunted buffalo with it. Just Apaches. After the army let him go he had hunted them for the bounty on their scalps. Then the rich old Mexican he had sold the scalps to down in Sonora, had died and he had turned to rustling. Now it looked like he was man-hunting again—and a white man should be easy to bag after hunting Apaches. Most of the men the old Mexican had hired to kill Apaches had been killed by Apaches. Whitey had survived and he wasn't worried about the man called Bowdry.

If he had only known what he was up against.

Whitey had approximately four hours left to live. He used up one of those hours on the ride north through the rocky, eroded hills toward the old Pollard shack. Two more hours he used up waiting until dark. Then, leaving his horse in a thicket a good mile away, he began his cautious approach on foot, the Ethan Allen at the ready, his thumb on the right hammer.

There was no moon yet and it was pitch dark. The low black trees stirred in a wind that had started blowing at sundown—the hour when winds normally died down. Whitey saw this as a bad sign, and was tempted to turn back. But he had the feeling that by now everyone at the 3-Bar would know what he was up to, and if he returned empty-handed he would look like a fool. Also, while the wind made him uneasy, it would help to cover his approach, as both movement and sound would be harder to detect with the trees and shrubs tossing and rattling their branches.

Nevertheless, he moved very slowly, a careful step at a time, and stopped often behind a rock or shrub to watch and listen. In a dark narrow valley between two steep rocky slopes he stood motionless for a full fifteen minutes, a strange chill creeping over him. The wind had turned cold, but not that cold, and it did not explain the tightness in his chest, the difficulty he had in breathing.

Once in the Chiricahua Mountains of Arizona he had felt this way when he was stalking a bad Apache, a renegade who was feared and hated even by his own people. Whitey had somehow known that the Apache was close by, and that if he moved the Apache would kill him. So he had not moved. He had remained utterly motionless the rest of the night, and sometime before dawn the Apache had slipped away, unseen and unheard. But Whitey had found his sign.

Well, he could not remain here all night. When the moon came up he would be exposed, if there was someone nearby.

He started to move on toward the next rock—and there it was again, that strange, paralyzing chill, that invisible hand of fear choking his breath away. He had not seen or heard anything to explain it, but his highly developed sixth sense warned him of a danger greater than he had ever faced, even when hunting Apaches.

He froze. He wanted desperately to hurl himself behind the nearest rock, but he knew that would give him away. And he thought it possible that the enemy—whoever he was—had not yet seen or heard him. So after a moment he crept on toward that black rock ahead of him.

There was nothing to warn him. No movement. No click of a gun hammer being drawn back. Just a sudden stab of flame from the black shadows, a deafening roar, the numbing shock of the bullet hitting him like a lead fist.

The next thing he knew he was lying on the hard rocky ground and the shadowy form of a man was bending over him, picking up the shotgun and removing the shells from his pockets, wasting no time or motions. A moment later, Whitey saw him moving silently away through the windy trees. Then the man faded into the darkness and—for Whitey—the darkness too vanished.

Bowdry heard the shot but did not investigate until daylight. It did not take him long to find the dead man. Backtracking him to the horse tied in the thicket, he found a box with half a dozen shotgun shells in the saddlebag. He took the shells but found nothing else he could use. Then he led the horse to the dead man, tied him across the saddle and sent the horse toward the 3-Bar with a whack across the rump.

That done, he went to work on the other man's trail. As expected, it was more difficult, and took more time. But finally he found where the man had left his horse back out of sight in some rocks and brush. Judging by the droppings and other signs, the horse had been there for some time, perhaps three or four hours.

That brought a look of worry to Bowdry's blue eyes. The horse had come from the direction of town and gone back that way, but he did not try to follow the horse. He was more interested in where the man had been for so long while the horse was tied here.

Returning to the spot where he had found the dead man, Bowdry tried to back-track the killer. But at this he had no luck. Before the shooting the man had been even more careful to leave no trail than afterwards, probably because he had more time then.

There was a look of puzzlement in Bowdry's eyes as he headed back toward the Pollard shack. Whoever the man was, he was waging a secret, deadly war on the Wadley outfit. But he was doing it for reasons of his own, not just to help Bowdry out. In fact, he was using Bowdry, letting him take the blame for all the killings. If the law ever came after anyone, it would be Bowdry.

But right now it appeared that it was the Wadleys who were coming after him—the whole bunch. He saw them coming through the trees not more than a hundred yards away. There were at least a dozen of them—and one was leading the dead man's horse with the body still across the saddle. They must have already been heading this way and picked the horse up en route.

The moment he caught a glimpse of them, Bowdry stepped behind a rock and watched them through some brush. They came straight on at a trot as if they had not seen him. The big paunchy man in the lead, on a flame-red horse, would be Rufe Wadley, and the plump grinning young man riding beside him was Gord Wadley. Some of those behind bore a slight resemblance to the two brothers, though none of them were as fat. The two Wadleys looked huge in the saddle but would be fairly short on the ground, for they both had stunted-looking bowlegs.

Bowdry did not move until they were close enough to see him behind the rock. Then he stood up a little straighter and trained the shotgun on them, though he kept the stock at waist level and merely raised the barrels, with his thumb on the hammers. He grinned a little at their surprise as they drew up, one white-haired old man glaring at him with wide startled black eyes.

"That's about far enough," he said quietly.

Rufe Wadley's face got a little pale behind the freckles, but his voice was strong and loud. "We was on our way to town. We wasn't aimin' to pay you no visit today, though I been thinkin' about it."

"You got business in town that needs so many men?" Bowdry asked, scanning the hard faces and cold eyes.

Rufe Wadley's mouth fell open and his small red eyes peered worriedly at the gunfighter. "Well, actually we was lookin' for Whitey there. When he didn't come back to the ranch last night, we decided to get a early start this mornin' and look for him. We figgered he was dead or hurt bad."

"Then when you found his horse and him across it you decided to go on to town and show everyone some more of my dirty work and tell them what good innocent boys you all are and how it ain't safe to ride the trails anymore because I'm liable to bushwhack you," Bowdry finished for him. "Tell me, what was Whitey doing sneaking around over here in the dark."

"I don't rightly know," Rufe Wadley said, getting angry and red in the face. "But I didn't know he was comin' over here. He never said nothin' to me about it. Never said nothin' to nobody."

Bowdry studied the big man silently, his eyes cold.

"I can see you don't believe me," Rufe Wadley growled. "Well, it don't matter none what you think. After all the killin' you've done, for no reason, you deserve whatever happens to you."

"For no reason!" Bowdry echoed.

"Whatever you think, we never killed that old man," Wadley told him. "We was just tryin' to scare him off."

"And if that didn't work, what then?" Bowdry asked.

Rufe Wadley's little eyes shifted away, but only for a moment. "I hadn't thought that far ahead yet. If I'd of knowed it was gonna cause so much trouble, I never would of bothered with him. We need that water, but it's so hard for cattle to get to where it's at, it ain't worth much."

"It's not worth what it'll cost you," Bowdry told him.

"It ain't worth what it's already cost," Rufe Wadley retorted, his eyes damp and his great voice shaking with bitter rage. "One of them boys you killed was my brother."

Bowdry nodded grimly. "I figured he was. At the time I thought him and those other two had killed the old man and come back to get me. That sort of burned me up, and even if I was wrong, I figured they needed killing. But I didn't kill that one across the saddle there."

"We may not look very bright to you, Bowdry," Rufe Wadley rumbled. "But we ain't fools. I ain't nohow."

Bowdry shrugged. "I didn't figure you'd believe it. But I'm not the only enemy you've got around here. I don't know who it is, but somebody's trying to kill off some of you boys and letting everyone think it's me."

Some of the men grunted in derision and a light-haired, green-eyed man—Clete Anson—asked angrily, "Just how stupid you think we are, Bowdry? I was over here the day you shot Pink Deeble, when we was just ridin' along mindin' our own business, on our way back to the ranch."

"I was with them too," Gord Wadley said.

"Did you see me shoot him?" Bowdry asked.

"Hell no," Gord Wadley said. "You stayed hid in the rocks and never give us no chance at you."

Bowdry shook his head, but did not say anything. It seemed that more talk would be a waste of time.

Rufe Wadley was studying him thoughtfully. "If you didn't kill

Whitey, who did?"

"I don't know," Bowdry said. "But I intend to find out. I can do my own killing—and I do enough without getting blamed for somebody else's."

"You shore do," Rufe Wadley barked. "Even if you didn't kill Whitey, you killed my brother—and that's enough for me. Now you gonna either have to use that scattergun or let us go on our way. You may get some of us, but you won't get us all."

"I didn't intend to use it unless I had to," Bowdry said. "Not today anyhow. But in the future I advise you to keep to the road and not take any shortcuts through here. If I see any of you around here after this, I'll take it to mean you've come after me, and I'll shoot first and ask questions later."

"Hell, that's what you been doin' all the time," Gord Wadley said.

"Shut up, Gord," Rufe Wadley said. He held the reins in his fat fist, studying Bowdry with hard eyes. "I ain't figgered out yet how I'm gonna do it, but I aim to see you pay for what you done to Hunk and them others. This wasn't none of yore business any of the time. It was between us and that old fool who didn't have sense enough to get out while he could, and you had to come in here and take sides with him agin' us. It wasn't even us shot him, but you had to go and kill a bunch of us. Well, you better enjoy these next few days. They could be yore last."

"Better let it drop before anybody else gets killed," Bowdry said.

"Let it drop, hell," Rufe Wadley snorted. "I aim to see you dead no matter how many more of us has to die first."

With that he kicked the red horse into a fast trot and the others followed closely behind him, looking back at Bowdry until they were out of sight.

CHAPTER 9

Emerging from the hotel lobby with his blanket roll tucked under his arm, Miles Hinton felt a stir of annoyance when he found the usual group of old men whittling on the veranda. Whittling and talking. They never stopped talking. Just like old women, he thought.

Old Doc Batter, the biggest talker among them, looked up and said, "How you doin', young feller? Hear you quit your job."

"They don't really need a desk clerk. Mr. Stewart said it looked like he was going to have to let me go if business didn't soon pick up." Hinton shrugged. "I quit so he wouldn't have to fire me."

He spoke quietly and courteously from habit. But the old-timers shifted uneasily when he turned his large pale eyes on them. To them he was just a nice quiet young man who had come to Gray Buttes a while back and gone to work in the hotel. They didn't know anything else about him. They never admitted it, even among themselves, but they didn't like him. He made them uncomfortable. Those fish-cold eyes, so round and unblinking and expressionless when he turned them on you. But it was more than that. It was a feeling they got around him.

Miles Hinton was aware of their dislike and discomfort, and it annoyed him. Once he had asked Mr. Stewart why he let them whittle on the veranda all the time and make a mess, when they did not stay at the hotel or even eat there very often, but Mr. Stewart had told him just to leave them be, they didn't mean any harm. But Hinton did not like it. He did not like them there all the time. All that stupid talk.

"What you aim to do now?" old Doc Batter asked. Batter was not there as much as the others, but he made up for it when he was there. That little old man simply never stopped talking, and unlike most westerners he was nosy as hell. "You aim to stay around a while, maybe look for another job, or ride on?"

"I haven't decided yet," Hinton said, politely enough, though he wanted to tell the old man it was none of his business. "I want to just take it easy for a few days. Get out in the fresh air more. Do some riding."

The old doctor glanced at his bone-handled Colt. "And catch up on your target practice? I hear you're real handy with that there gun."

Hinton shrugged, still distantly polite. "It's a way to pass the time."

"That's a real nice lookin' gun," Doc Batter said. "What is that, a .45?"

".44," Hinton said. "Well, I guess I'll see you gentlemen when I get back. I may decide to camp out, if the spirit moves me. That's why I'm taking my blankets and a bite to eat."

"If you run into that Gord Wadley out there anywhere, tell him I need my shotgun to go huntin' with," old Doc Batter said, reaching for his flask. "But I don't guess it'll do no good. I prob'ly won't ever see that gun again."

"I've got a feeling you're right," Hinton said, stepping off the veranda.

They watched him go down the dusty hard-packed street toward the stable, and one of the old-timers said, "Fool boy don't even know how to roll up his blankets. Notice how long that roll is?"

"He sure looks different with that hat and gun on, though, don't he? If he didn't look so much like a dude in them fancy duds, I'd figger he was a gunfighter."

"He may be," Doc Batter said, lowering his flask and staring after the former desk clerk. "I hear he's real good with that gun."

"Where did you hear that, Doc?" asked a grinning old whittler who had neither hat nor hair on his head. "I don't know anyone who's seen him shoot. He was the one said he only takes that gun along to shoot targets. Maybe he wears it 'cause he's scared of them Wadleys."

"Can't say I blame him," old Doc Batter said, taking another pull at this flask. "I believe I told you boys what a close call I had out there the other day."

Hinton, meanwhile, had reached the livery stable. He waited while the old hostler saddled his sorrel gelding, then tied the blanket roll behind the cantle himself. Stepping into the saddle, he left town and headed south, into the deadly hills where few dared to ride.

He had gone about a mile at a leisurely jog trot, when he suddenly reined aside into a clump of trees and watched the Wadley outfit go by on the road to town. It appeared to be the whole bunch plus three new men he had not seen before and the dead man bouncing along across his saddle. Then Hinton searched his memory and decided one man was missing—Pink Deeble, the bullet-scratched man whose life old Doc Batter claimed to have saved.

A smile gleamed briefly in Hinton's glassy gray eyes. This would be a good time to finish that little piece of work, while the others were away. It would be ironical if Deeble got blasted this time with Doc Batter's own gun.

He waited until the 3-Bar men were indistinct in the dust and distance toward town. Then he got back in the trail and rode on south. When the trail forked, he took the fork that led toward the LR. If the Wadleys noticed his tracks on their way back, they would think the tracks had been made by Josh Larkin or someone on the way to Lucy Reardon's small ranch out in the hills, and they would think no more about it.

Lucy Reardon. Hinton's pale eyes were oddly dreamy as he rode on into the bright morning, the sun shining yellow and warm on the cedar-dotted, boulder-strewn hills. He was tempted to ride on out to her ranch, or near there, just in hopes of getting a distant glimpse of her. He had seen her only a few times in town and had never spoken to her—but in his mind he saw her often and sometimes he carried on imaginary conversations with her. Most women did not interest him much—but most women did not look like her. That long red hair, those fantastic curves… he wiped his sweaty right hand on his trousers—a hand that never sweated when it held a gun.

He put her from his mind and turned off the trail, circling around the old Pollard shack hidden in the rocks and then lining out on a straight course for the 3-Bar. If the Wadleys back-tracked him it would look as if he had come directly from the Pollard place, but they would lose his trail on rocky ground before they got there.

It did not bother him that Bowdry would be blamed for what he did. Bowdry had already killed so many men, what did it matter if he got credit for a few he had not killed? The law—if it ever closed in—could hang him no higher, the Wadleys could only kill him once. No matter how you looked at it, Bowdry was doomed. And Hinton figured that he was doing the man a big favor by eliminating some of his enemies. Because of him, there was a slim chance that Bowdry might even come out of this business alive. But Hinton did not really care much one way or the other. Bowdry meant nothing to him.

At last he halted on a cedar hill overlooking the 3-Bar. He studied the deserted looking buildings and corrals for a time, then untied the blanket roll from behind the saddle, removed the shotgun and made a shorter, neater roll this time. The long-barreled shotgun was in two pieces. He put it together and loaded it, then got back in the saddle and walked his horse silently down the slope through the rocks and stunted cedars.

He left the sorrel behind the windowless bunkhouse, went around front and pushed the door open. "Anybody here?" he called.

Pink Deeble sat up on a filthy bunk and brushed dead-looking pale hair away from his pink eyes. His shirt was unbuttoned and a dirty white bandage could be seen on his scrawny chest. "Just me," he said in a hollow voice. "The others has all gone to look fur a man that didn't come back last night." He took a closer look at Hinton framed in the doorway, his weak eyes blinking at the bright light outside. He could not make out Hinton's features clearly. "I don't believe I've seen you around before. You lookin' fur work?"

Hinton shook his head, smiling faintly. "No, I'd rather ride the grubline. It's easier."

Pink Deeble buttoned his shirt. "I was just fixin' to stir up a bite to eat, then I dozed off again. I been doin' the cookin' the last few days. We ain't had no reg'lar cook around here since Bertha Wadley run off with Moose Grogan. But her name wasn't Wadley atter she married up with Clete Anson. She used to cook fur the whole outfit, not that she ever liked it much. Since she left we been takin' turns. It wasn't my turn, but somebody tuck a shot at me the other day."

He peered at Hinton and noticed the shotgun in his hand, held down along his leg. His eyes almost leapt from their sockets and his face, already pale, went sickly white with dread. Yet he made a desperate attempt to appear calm and casually unconcerned, as if he had not recognized the shotgun and did not know that Hinton must have killed Whitey to get it.

He got carefully to his feet, saying with only a slight tremor in his voice, "I'll see if I can rustle us some grub. I could use a bite my own self."

He reached for his hat, while Hinton looked on in cold amusement. Deeble's belt and gun hung on the bunk post just below his hat. When his hand was almost to the hat, it suddenly dipped toward the walnut butt of the gun. But it would not have mattered what he did. He would have died in any case. He just hastened his end a little by grabbing for the hogleg.

Miles Hinton brought up the shotgun and emptied both barrels at him in one deafening roar, splattering him all over the place. Pink Deeble never knew what hit him.

The late Whitey had been right. At close range, birdshot would tear a man up pretty bad.

There were several horses in the corral. Hinton ran them out, drove them off and scattered them, losing his own tracks among theirs. But one of the horses, a sorrel that looked much like his own, he hazed on into the hills. He drove the horse into a distant wash, shot it and caved earth and rocks in on top of it. To the casual eye it would look like a section of the bank had given away because of the undercutting of water in the rainy season.

When the Wadley men returned, the first thing they noticed was the corral bars down and the horses gone.

"That goddamn Pink," Gord Wadley said. "He musta left the bars down."

"Pink!" Rufe Wadley roared, turning in the saddle to glare about. Then he noticed the bunkhouse door open. He rode across to the bunkhouse, bent over in the saddle and peered inside. "Get over here!"

They came on the run, some on horses and some on foot, and swarmed into the bunkhouse. Clete Anson's cry of outrage could be heard above the excited babble of voices. Clete had been quite fond of Pink Deeble, the near albino. "Birdshot! That bastard come here while we was gone and blasted Pink with that shotgun he took off Whitey! I knowed all the time it was him killed Whitey!"

"Shut up!" Rufe Wadley roared, lest anyone forget he was still doing the thinking and giving the orders. "Two of you stay here and scrub him off the floor! Rest of you hit the saddle!"

"Hell, he's all over the walls too," someone said. "It'll take more'n two."

That one and two more stayed behind. The others galloped after the stolen horses. Rufe Wadley's face was purple with a gathering rage. His voice was hoarse. "Now he's stealin' my horses!"

"Hell, we stole 'em," Gord Wadley said, grinning.

"Shut up!" Rufe Wadley shouted.

The horse tracks soon scattered, and Clete Anson said, "It was just a trick!"

"Hell, I figgered all along it was," Gord Wadley said, the usual grin on his red face.

"You never figgered anything of the kind," Rufe Wadley snorted. "You ain't got brains enough. And you shore as hell wouldn't of waited this long to say somethin'."

"Now we don't know which tracks to foller," Clete Anson said in disgust. "But it don't matter. We know where he went. He's back up in them rocks by now. We should of back-tracked him."

Rufe Wadley glanced at the new men. "What do you boys think?"

They merely shrugged, looking off in the general direction the horses had gone.

Old Bones Grogan's eyes were damp and bitter. "I wish Moose was here. He'd know what to do."

Rufe Wadley snorted at that. He was in a very bad mood, and

running short of patience. Everything seemed to be going wrong lately and he seemed powerless to do anything about it, what with the kind of help he had. "Moose, hell," he said. "Moose is dead because he didn't have enough brains to get in out of the rain."

Old Bones Grogan threw him a startled look, shocked by such talk. But when he saw the wild look in Rufe's eyes, he kept his resentment to himself and trembled in silent anger.

"Well, let's round up the horses and decide later what to do about Bowdry," Rufe said in disgust.

He himself returned to the ranch and let the others round up the horses. Gord came in later and told him they had found them all except one. "Looks like Bowdry stole that blaze-face sorrel."

CHAPTER 10

"What the hell?"

Bowdry, though not normally a man who talked to himself, expressed a grunt of surprise when he heard the clatter of fast-approaching horses beyond the west ridge, and what sounded like a feminine yell for help.

He was standing in the rocks on the east ridge, the shotgun cradled in his arms. Facing around, he saw Lucy Reardon fanning her brightly colored pinto down the opposite slope toward the old shack. Josh Larkin was not far behind on his equally colorful Appaloosa, hollering at her. She hollered at Bowdry, unseen in the rocks. But she must have figured that was where he would be, for she came on past the shack at a gallop, still yelling his name.

When she was almost to the waterhole, the pinto stepped in a hole and turned a neat little somersault. Lucy Reardon flew a short piece through the air like a bird that has not yet learned to fly, arms and legs frantically flapping, long red hair streaming behind. She landed with a loud unladylike grunt, the breath knocked out of her. But she came up fast and ran screaming for the rocks to escape the pounding hoofs of the Appaloosa, now almost on top of her, a thousand pounds of excited animal frenzy.

Josh Larkin yelled an incoherent cry of rage and dived off on top of her. Down she went again with a louder scream, but came up spitting dust and clawing and shrieking like a wildcat. Larkin scrambled back with arms up to protect his face.

Bowdry sighed. It seemed that the human comedy got funnier all the time. But at the moment the pair down there appeared human in form only.

He turned to scan the valley to the east and the cedar slope beyond, ignoring the yells and screams behind him. He was not a man with much faith left and the thought had occurred to him that this might be a trick to divert his attention away from danger approaching in some other direction. But he soon dismissed the notion and went unhurriedly down through the rocks to the waterhole, bent down for a drink, then rose and stood watching the fight, grinning a little until they noticed him. Then he looked as sober as a judge.

Josh Larkin backed off and dropped his hands when he saw Bowdry. Lucy Reardon stood in a crouch, right hand fisted, the left out like a claw, her white teeth bared in a kind of snarl. She looked like she was just getting started good, while Larkin was sweating and heaving as if he had had to run her pinto down on foot, before the fight even began.

"You need any help?" Bowdry asked him.

"Who, me?" Larkin asked, his cow-country drawl in no way impaired by his excitement. "Hell no, I don't need no help. I just come atter her to fetch her on back to the LR where she belongs."

Lucy Reardon did not seem much excited either. Apparently it was a game they were used to playing. She was almost smiling as she said, "I ain't going back with you, you bastard." But then her eyes suddenly blazed with anger. "I ain't going back till you get your junk out of my house and your cows off my range!"

"I'll leave when I'm ready," Larkin told her, fingering a small cut at the corner of his mouth. " 'Sides, most of them cows is mine anyhow."

"Ha!" she said. "You stole 'em!"

"I reckon you ought to know," the big rustler replied. "It was mainly yore idea. All that talk about how we could have us a big herd in no time. How we could be partners with nobody the wiser, and how we wouldn't even have to change the brand 'cause LR could stand for

Larkin and Reardon just as easy as it could for Lucy Reardon."

She shot Bowdry an uneasy glance, then said angrily to the big-toothed man before her, "You're lying! That's all you ever do, is tell lies. Biggest liar I ever saw."

Josh Larkin's mouth fell open in a look of genuine surprise. "Look who's talkin'! When it comes to tellin' lies, I ain't even in the same stall with you! You said you was just gonna ride down to check on that waterhole, but I knowed which waterhole you was headin' for, all right!"

"So you had to foller me, like always," she said with biting scorn. "Always sneaking around and spying on me."

Bowdry threw an uneasy look over his shoulder, then said with sudden impatience, "You two finish that somewhere else."

Josh Larkin took exception to his tone. He reddened with anger and gave the gunfighter a mean look. "I got just as much right to be here as you have. This place don't belong to you. It never even belonged to old man Pollard, and it shore as hell don't belong to you. It's just as much mine as it is yores."

"You can have it after I'm gone," Bowdry said, his blue eyes turning to ice. "If you're still alive then."

Josh Larkin snorted. "You mean if you're still alive!"

"If it's a fight you want—"

Larkin bristled like an angry dog. "Yeah, what if it is?" he snapped.

"—I'm pretty busy with the Wadleys, but I guess I can spare a few minutes for you."

The gunfighter was entirely too quiet and calm about the whole thing, and Larkin did not like the icy chill in the steady blue eyes. The big rustler suddenly turned toward his horse, saying over his shoulder, "I didn't come over here lookin' for no trouble. I just come atter her." The Appaloosa stood ground-hitched nearby, having stopped in its tracks an instant after Larkin left the saddle. Larkin stepped astride and sat looking at Lucy Reardon with a mixture of lingering anger and desperation in his eyes. "You comin' or not?"

She stood with hands on hips, gazing back at him in gloating triumph. "What do you think, big man?" she jeered. She stuck out her tongue at him and made a very unladylike sound.

Larkin flushed red. He started to get back down off his horse, then glanced at the silent Bowdry and changed his mind. "You aim to stay over here with him?" he asked Lucy.

"I'll do whatever I please!" she said defiantly.

"We'll see about that," Josh Larkin told her, his jaws clenched and his face so red it looked like it might explode. He turned the Appaloosa and put it up the steep slope through the rocks at a reckless gallop, which was the only way he ever seemed to ride.

Lucy Reardon stood looking after him, her expression altering to one of worry. "He's headed straight for the 3-Bar," she said.

"After some help?" Bowdry asked.

She nodded. "If he can't get me back one way, he will another."

"I thought he was about ready to declare war on the 3-Bar. Eliminate the competition."

Lucy Reardon glanced at him. "Right now you're the only competition he's worried about."

Bowdry stared at her with hard eyes. "I sure don't know why you were running from him or yelling for help. It should've been the other way around. Why were you headed this way anyhow? I mean, before he took out after you?"

She shrugged. "I wanted to see how you're doing. And I thought you might like to talk to someone about all this trouble you're in."

Bowdry shook his head. "I'm not in any trouble. They're the ones who're in trouble. I don't mean to brag, but those boys are outclassed. They should have stuck to rustling and picking on old men."

"I thought they'd picked on the wrong old man," Lucy Reardon said. "You're Will Pollard, ain't you? He told me about you."

Bowdry once more shook his head. "My name's Bowdry. That old man was a little weak in the head. He seemed to think I was his son and I just let him think it. I've heard of Will Pollard, but I'm not him."

"You sure about that?" she asked, watching him skeptically.

Bowdry frowned slightly. "You think whatever you like. It won't do any good for me to keep repeating it."

"If you ain't him, why are you here?" Lucy asked. "Did Harris Thacker send you?"

"I never saw Harris Thacker. But if what I've heard is true, he could have hired me pretty cheap."

"What did you hear?"

"What everyone's heard, I guess."

"You mean about the Wadleys forcing him to sign his ranch over to them and then running him out of the country?"

Bowdry merely nodded, his eyes cold.

"So that's why you're doing it," she said. "You don't like the idea of them getting away with that. But what can you do against all of them?"

"They're getting fewer all the time," Bowdry said.

"Don't bet on it," she said. "That's a hangout for every rustler and outlaw for two or three hundred miles, and I think the Wadleys have got some more relatives back in Texas or someplace."

"They'll never get here in time to do this bunch much good."

Lucy Reardon studied the gunfighter thoughtfully. "You must be joking. There's at least a dozen tough, mean men over there. Everybody around here's scared of them."

"I ain't," Bowdry said. "I've met their kind before. They ain't near as tough as they sound."

"And now that crazy Josh will probably throw in with them because of me," Lucy said worriedly. "I never thought about him pulling a stunt like that. But I just know that's where he's gone."

Bowdry frowned in annoyance. His voice was even quieter than usual but it had a rough edge to it. "Dammit, I asked you to stay away from over here. I told you I already had enough trouble. But you had to play games, trying to make fools out of him and me too." He suddenly looked sharply at her. "Is that what's been going on all along? You'd come hightailing it over here every time you and Larkin had a little spat, letting on like you needed that old man to protect you? Is that how it was?"

She looked away, her sunburnt freckled face even redder than usual. "No! What gave you that idea?"

Bowdry's frown deepened as he watched her. "How much of the time did you stay over here anyway?"

She flashed him an angry look. "That's none of your business! If you ain't Will Pollard, then that old man wasn't anything to you, and you ain't got no right to ask me all these questions."

"Who I am ain't important," Bowdry said. "Who killed that old man—that's what's important."

There was a sudden look of anguish on Lucy Reardon's face. But she was not looking at Bowdry or paying any attention to his words. "Oh no," she said softly.

Bowdry turned. The pinto was limping about with a broken ankle, nickering softly in pain.

"Oh my God!" Lucy Reardon said. "That bastard made me ruin my horse. Now he'll have to be killed."

"Not here," Bowdry said. "There'll be enough buzzards swarming around here without a dead horse."

"Oh, the hell with you!" Lucy Reardon cried, going toward the pinto.

But in the end she let him lead the badly limping horse over the east ridge and shoot it so far away that she barely heard the shot.

When he came back she was sitting on the ground near the waterhole, hugging her knees. "That was the best horse I ever had," she said.

Bowdry looked at her in surprise, but said nothing. Like most western men, he did not have much use for pintos. But Indians and women of all races seemed to like them.

"Well, I liked him the best," she said after a time.

"You can't stay here," Bowdry said quietly. "I don't know when the Wadleys may show up. You can take the old man's roan. I'll saddle him for you."

"I'm not going," she said, looking toward the old shack with empty eyes.

Bowdry looked sharply at her. "What do you mean, you're not going?"

"Just that," she said. "I'm staying here."

"Like hell. I'm sorry about your horse, I'm sorry about Larkin, I'm sorry about everything. But you can't stay here. I can't worry about you and the Wadleys at the same time."

"You don't have to worry about me," she said. "I can take care of myself. And I can handle a gun. You're going to need some help, especially if Josh comes back with them. He knows this place a lot better than they do, maybe even better than you do. He knows all the hiding places, all the trails in and out. When I was over here he used to sneak around in them rocks spying on us. Sometimes at night he'd even sneak down and try to peek through the window. I don't know what the jealous fool expected to see."

"You mean he'd come down on foot?" Bowdry asked.

She nodded. "Sometimes he'd leave his horse way back over there on the other side of that ridge, so we wouldn't hear it if it whinnied or anything."

Bowdry squatted on his heels near her and leaned on the Greener, thinking about what she had said. "He was here the night the old man was killed. He told me he came here looking for you."

She glanced quickly at Bowdry and then looked away. "I wasn't even here that night. I just went for a ride. But I guess he thought I was over here."

After a moment Bowdry asked, "Do you think he could have killed the old man?"

Lucy crossed her arms, hugging herself as if she had a chill. "I don't know," she said. "You don't think it was the Wadleys?"

"At first I just took for granted it was them, or one of them. I saw three of them in town that night and I figured they stopped on the way home, back over there a piece, and one of them rode over here and shot the old man. I only found the tracks of one horse—and it turned out to be the tracks of Larkin's Appaloosa. But he swore he didn't kill the old man and just about convinced me he was telling the truth. If he wasn't, he's one of the best liars I ever ran across."

"He's that all right," Lucy said. She thought for a moment, then shook her head. "I just don't know. I know he didn't like me to come over here, and I guess I made it worse by teasing him about it. I thought it was funny the way he's get so mad and jealous. And it was sort of funny too the way that old man was scared of him but determined to protect me with his own life if necessary. I never thought for a minute that I was in any real danger, but I didn't let on. That would have spoiled it, and if Mr. Pollard had ever caught on, he probably wouldn't have let me stay over here when Josh was having one of his spells. Of course, that would have been just what Josh wanted, for Mr. Pollard to make me leave. That's the only reason I did it, to spite Josh. I sure never thought it would end up the way it did. I mean, if Josh did kill him."

"Everything points at him," Bowdry said. "But in spite of that, I've got a feeling it was somebody else."

"Who?"

"I wish I knew."

CHAPTER 11

Josh Larkin headed straight for the 3-Bar, his face red with rage. The Appaloosa flashed through the bleak gray country, leaving a streak of dust. He galloped into the yard unmindful of the alarm he spread among the itchy-fingered outfit and strode up to the door like he had rights.

Rufe Wadley sat ponderously behind the office desk trying, as usual, to look important. His bloated red face registered shock and indignation at Larkin's unceremonious entrance.

"What the hell you mean chargin' in here like that? Don't you know that's a good way to get shot?"

"You boys shore ain't had much luck shootin' nobody so far," Larkin drawled. "Unless it was old man Pollard."

"That wasn't us," Rufe Wadley snapped. "I figgered it was you."

"It shore as hell wasn't me," Larkin said. "I reckon Bowdry thinks it was. But I don't give a damn what he thinks."

"What can I do for you?" Rufe Wadley asked impatiently.

"It ain't what you can do for me," Larkin told him. "It's what I can do for you."

Bowdry led both horses down through the rocks to the waterhole, took a long drink himself and filled his canteen. Then he led the horses on to the corral, turned the roan into the corral and tightened the cinch of the brown horse's saddle.

Lucy Reardon came to the door of the shack. "You're putting the horses back in the corral?" she asked.

"Just the roan," he said. "He'll be handy if you decide to use him."

"You mean you're leaving?" she asked in surprise.

He turned and regarded her with black eyes. "You ain't leaving me much choice," he said. "I can't make you leave, so I'll have to."

"You think that will keep them from attacking?" she asked. "They won't even know you're gone."

He nodded, watching her with his blue eyes half closed against the sunlight. "I wouldn't hang around here if I were you. It wouldn't serve any purpose with me gone, would it?"

"So that's it," she said, her face reddening behind the freckles. "It's just a trick to get rid of me!"

Bowdry shrugged. "Call it what you like. I don't think of it as a trick myself. I just don't intend to stay here if you aim to. Nothing personal, but when I go into a fight I don't want to be worried about a woman getting shot. I'm liable to get myself shot worrying about you."

"I wouldn't want that to happen," she said in a quiet, dead tone. "I thought I could help you."

If anything, Bowdry's face got harder. "The only way you can help me is by getting the hell out of here," he said.

"All right," she said wearily. "If that's what you want. But I reckon you know they'll burn this old house if they don't find anyone here, to keep you from coming back."

Bowdry shrugged. "It don't mean anything to me. I imagine it means more to them than it does to me. This would be a good place to hide out and fort up, with enough men to defend it. My guess is that's one reason they want it. And by now they know I'm usually up in the rocks anyway, so it wouldn't serve any purpose to burn it down."

"Are you going to stay if I leave?" Lucy asked.

"I'm not going to be here all the time," Bowdry said. "I'll be riding around some."

"I had a bite to eat about ready." Lucy Reardon said. "You might as well eat something before you go off anywhere."

"Wish I could," he said. "But I'm sort of in a hurry right now. If you want to leave something for me, I may come back for it later. But I wish you wouldn't hang around here much longer."

She studied his craggy face. "You ain't thinking about leaving for good, are you?" she asked.

Bowdry's lips twisted in a faint smile as he stepped into the saddle. Without another word he turned the brown horse and headed for the east ridge.

When he got in the high rocks near the crest, Bowdry halted and looked back. He turned the gelding around and watched the house from a point where he himself would not be seen, unless it was by a lazily circling buzzard on the lookout for fresh meat. "Not here, you bastard," Bowdry muttered. "I left you a horse, two hills over." Then he forgot about the bird as Lucy Reardon left the shack moving quickly toward the corral. Wasting no time, she caught and saddled the roan and rode over the west ridge while Bowdry watched with a faintly ironical smile. She had decided that she didn't want to be here alone when the Wadleys showed up, perhaps led by vindictive Josh Larkin. It appeared that she was not as crazy as Bowdry had begun to think.

He turned the dark horse, rode over the crest and down through the rocks to the valley below. An old trail ran along this narrow valley and then along the rim of the canyon that was actually a box canyon, ending abruptly against the steep rocky hill that guarded the Pollard shack on the south. Bowdry rode across the overgrown trail and put the horse up the long cedar slope beyond.

Just ahead of him now was the spot where Pink Deeble had been shot by the man with the bone-handled Colt. Sliding the shotgun from the scabbard, Bowdry loped past the spot and weaved through the rocks and low cedars until he reached the top of the hill. Here he stopped and looked off to the south.

Three riders were coming along the road from the 3-Bar a half mile away, and even at that distance he saw that one of the horses was Josh Larkin's Appaloosa. The other two appeared to be bays or sorrels, but they were still too far off to tell anything about the riders.

Bowdry pulled back off the hilltop and tied his horse out of sight in some trees. Then, taking the Greener, he made his way on foot to a jumble of rocks and brush near the old wagon road that wound along the back side of the slope. From here he could not see the riders coming, just as they would not be able to see him, and he heard them talking before he heard the trotting horses. Josh Larkin had a rather loud drawling voice, well suited to the outdoors, but not so well suited to his present purpose.

"You two go on around to the north side and git in them rocks with yore rifles. I'll ride down to the shack and call him down into the open where you can git a good shot at him. Just don't miss, dammit, or he's liable to git mad and plug me."

Gord Wadley also had a drawl all his own, easily distinguished though not as loud as Larkin's. "You mean you aim to ride in there from this side?"

"Yeah, I might as well. He seen me come this way, so it's the way he'll expect me to come back."

"Hell, if you go in that way, he won't never let you go all the way down to the shack where we can git a shot at him," Gord Wadley said. "If he's on this side, he'll stop you up there in them rocks where we can't even see him."

"I never thought of that," Josh Larkin said, and they pulled up in the road where Bowdry could see them. Larkin's mouth was open in a look of surprise, his big teeth showing. "I'll just have to go on around with you boys and come in from the west the way I usually do and ride on down to the shack 'fore he can stop me. Then I'll call him down out of them rocks where you two can see him." The big rustler grinned at Gord Wadley. "You ain't as dumb as you look, are you?"

"Heck no I ain't," Gord replied with the usually stupid grin on his fuzzy red face. He was still quite young, perhaps still in his teens. But about as old as he would ever be, the way he was going.

Larkin and Gord Wadley trotted on along the road abreast, and the silent third man followed them—it was the one with pale hair and glittering green eyes, Clete Anson. He had an old Colt revolving rifle in one hand, and Gord Wadley had a slightly newer Henry.

Bowdry waited until they were out of sight and sound, waited a few minutes longer to make sure, then ran for his horse. He jerked the reins free and leapt into the saddle, streaking back down the cedar slope at a gallop. He dipped into the narrow valley, scrambled up the ridge beyond, and left the horse in the rock-walled enclosure he used for a corral. Then he ran along the rocky ridge until it curved around to the west. Actually, this same ridge described a loop, enclosing the bowl and the house on three sides, but for purposes of defense he always thought of it as three separate ridges, east, north, and west, in that order. He halted in the rocks on the north ridge and saw them coming along an arroyo, still some distance off. They separated, Josh Larkin leaving the arroyo on his tireless Appaloosa and angling west, taking his time to give them plenty of time. As for Bowdry, he had time to catch his breath and pick himself a position near the head of the arroyo.

He stood the Greener against a rock and checked his pistols, keeping one in his hand, leaving the Greener where it was because he did not think he would need it. Not today. Not for Gord Wadley and Clete Anson.

They left their horses down below and lugged their rifles up the steep slope, the short fat Gord Wadley panting in the lead, more red-faced than usual, but displaying a cheerful grin. Perhaps he was already thinking about what he would tell the others when he got back to the 3-Bar with Bowdry's scalp for a souvenir. Clete Anson brought up the rear, silent and sinister, a wild look in his green eyes as he studied the rocks. The two were about as different from each other as two men could be, but here they were, with the same deadly purpose in mind.

Bowdry crouched behind some brush with a cocked revolver in his hand and watched them go right by him, so close he could smell their stale unwashed odor and hear their heavy breathing. They might have seen him, but they were not expecting him to be there. They halted between two outcroppings of bare rock near the peak, with a lower outcrop before them, and Gord Wadley said, "This here's a good place. And there comes old Josh," he added with a lopsided grin.

Bowdry stepped out behind them with the New Model leveled, the Russian still holstered. "Freeze," he said. "Don't even breathe till I tell you to."

Gord Wadley grunted in surprise. Clete Anson went into a tense crouch, gripping the old Colt revolving rifle in both hands, ready to swing it around.

"Don't try it," Bowdry advised him. "Even Hickok wasn't that good."

"Yeah, but Hickok didn't know there was nobody behind him though," Gord Wadley said. He was the type to find something to grin at whatever the occasion, apparently never believing anyone would shoot down a jolly young man like himself, just when he was reaching his full growth. Not even an intended victim like Bowdry would do that.

"Be quiet," Bowdry told him.

Down below, Josh Larkin trotted into view on this side of the shack and halted the Appaloosa in the open, looking toward the rocks on the east ridge. "Hey, Bowdry!" he called. "Come on down! I want to talk to you a minute!"

Gord Wadley and Clete Anson shifted uncomfortably, no doubt wanting to warn him, but silenced by Bowdry's gun at their backs.

"Let's see what you boys can do with those rifles," Bowdry told them.

They looked around at him in surprise, not certain they'd heard right.

"Just pretend that's me down there and you want to have a little fun," Bowdry said. "I don't mean for you to kill him—not that much fun. I just want you to scare him to death."

Clete Anson's pale green eyes glittered with hatred, but a sudden grin spread across Gord Wadley's red face as he shifted his glance back to Josh Larkin down by the shack.

"Hey, Bowdry!" Larkin called again.

Gord Wadley and Clete Anson began firing. Through the white smoke of their rifles Bowdry saw the bullets kick up dust around the nervous Appaloosa's feet. Josh Larkin threw a startled look at the rocks, gaping in shocked disbelief.

"Hey!" he cried. "What the hell!"

Gord Wadley chuckled, laid his fat cheek against the Henry and put a bullet so close to Larkin he must have heard it's angry little buzz.

"Sons of bitches!" he screamed, shaking his fist at the rocks. Then, afraid he had given himself away, he looked in alarm toward the east ridge where Bowdry usually was. "Don't shoot me, Bowdry! Them Wadleys is attackin'!" As he spoke he reined the Appaloosa around, disappeared briefly behind the shack and then galloped for the west ridge, bent low over the horse's neck.

Clete Anson lowered his empty rifle, but Gord Wadley continued to fire until the horse and rider dropped from sight beyond the ridge. Then he lowered the Henry and looked around with a grin, as if he and Bowdry had been pals all along and had even plotted this together. Bowdry, however, had a better memory.

"Put them down gently, boys, then shed the gunbelts."

They obeyed in silence, Gord Wadley still grinning, Clete Anson still watching for a chance to catch Bowdry off guard.

Bowdry regarded the pair with an absence of affection that bordered on active dislike. "I guess you boys were just hunting rabbits and got lost," he said.

"Yeah, that's what we was doin'," Gord Wadley said, and even Clete Anson looked at him with contempt for his simplicity.

"Like hell," Bowdry said. "You meant to plug me when I came down out of those rocks."

Gord Wadley looked uneasy for the first time, even a little embarrassed. "Well, you killed my brother," he said. "And all them others."

"I killed them because they came over here to get me," Bowdry said. "But the truth is I've sort of lost interest in you boys for the time being. The only one I'm interested in is the one who killed the old man, and I've about decided it wasn't any of your outfit."

"I know damn well it wasn't," Gord Wadley said.

Bowdry nodded. "That's why I'm letting you go. But this is the last time I'll be so generous. Tell that big fat brother of yours I just want to find out who killed the old man and I ain't got no time for you boys. If he's smart he'll let this die down while he's got a chance.

"But it don't really matter to me one way or the other. It's my honest opinion that all of you need killing. But the people who would profit most by your death—the sort who can't defend themselves—are just the ones who'd feel sorry for you bastards if you got what you deserve. Instead of thanking me, they'd likely get all worked up and come after me with a rope. They'd think you poor misguided boys should have been given another chance." Bowdry's cold blue eyes frosted over. "Another chance to go on doing what you've always done, which was whatever you thought you could get away with. Well, they're the ones who're going to have to put up with you after I'm gone. So I'd just as soon let them have it their way—unless you sorry sons of bitches force me to kill you."

"You may git some of us," Gord Wadley said, still not converted. "You won't git us all."

"It's beginning to look like I won't have to," Bowdry said. "I don't know who it is, but somebody besides me seems not to like you boys very much. That's one reason I'm letting you go, so you'll know I had a chance to kill you and didn't. If you've got any brains at all, that should tell you something."

"What?" Gord asked.

"It should tell you I'm not the man you should be worried about. So far I haven't shot anyone who didn't come asking for it. But if you boys keep hunting trouble, you're going to find it. Now get going before I change my mind. I'll keep your guns so you won't get any ideas about sneaking back right away."

Gord Wadley shrugged. "Them rifles wasn't ours nohow. We just borrowed them from some of the others."

"Then I don't guess you're out much, are you?" Bowdry said.

"Just them old handguns."

"A pretty small price to pay for your lives—don't you agree?"

Josh Larkin was waiting for them on the 3-Bar road, a big pistol in his hand and murder in his bright blue eyes.

"Last time we seen you, you was high-tailin' it toward the LR," Gord Wadley said, grinning at the memory. "That there shore is a fast horse."

"This here's a fast gun too," Josh Larkin told him. "How'd you sorry bastards like a demonstration?"

"Bowdry tuck our guns," Gord said uncomfortably. "He was waitin' up there like he knowed we was comin'. I guess he musta seen us. He made us do that shootin' back there. It wasn't our own idea."

"No, I don't reckon it was," Josh Larkin said. "You two never had a idea between you, unless somebody else thought of it first. I should of knowed Bowdry'd be too smart for you and get the drop on you."

"Hell, it looks like he was too smart for all of us," Gord Wadley said.

"I reckon he was, this time," Josh Larkin admitted. "Made us look like damn fools. But we shore as hell ain't finished with him. Not by a long shot."

CHAPTER 12

Gord Wadley and Clete Anson had brought no spare ammunition for the borrowed rifles, apparently figuring they wouldn't need it—as, indeed, they hadn't—and Bowdry had no powder and lead for the Colt revolving rifle. So he broke the old gun on a rock, despite its sturdy resistance. He kept the Henry, for the two dead Mexicans had carried long-barreled Colt revolvers that used the .44 Henry cartridge, with three belts of cartridges each. The confiscated pistols he hid in the rocks nearby, where they might be needed one day, but he took to carrying the Henry about with him—in addition to the Greener and his Smith & Wesson revolvers.

For he had little hope that the Wadleys would quit trying to kill him. They might come after him again at any time—and they might all come at once, with Josh Larkin egging them on. Out of crazy jealousy, Larkin had gone over to their side, and Bowdry had no friends, no one to help him.

Then he thought about the man who had killed Whitey and perhaps others.

Miles Hinton dismounted in front of the general store, tied his horse and went inside. "Box of .44s," he said to the gray-haired man behind the counter.

"Help yourself," Ollie Rice told him. "You know where they are— over there on the shelf."

As Hinton turned toward the shelf, Rice said, "Oh, by the way, you got a letter."

Hinton looked around in surprise. "A letter?"

"Yep. I'll go back here and get it. Take a minute. You go ahead and get the shells."

The storekeeper headed for the post office in a small room at the back, and Hinton took a box of .44 Colt centerfire cartridges from the shelf. He noticed several boxes of shotgun shells and studied them with interest. Glancing toward the back, he saw that Ollie Rice was still out of sight in the cubbyhole post office. Hinton took a box of 12-gauge buckshot and slipped it inside his coat, back up under his left arm where it would be less noticeable and where he could grip the box with his arm.

As he turned away from the wall of shelves, Ollie Rice emerged from the little post office, saying, "Here we are." He seemed to be looking at Hinton oddly as he came down the aisle between racks of dry goods and handed him the envelope. Hinton paid for the Colt cartridges and Ollie Rice watched him leave. Then the storekeeper went over to the shelves where the cartridges were and stood frowning at the empty place where the box of 12-gauge shells had been, then he turned to look through the window. But Hinton was already gone.

"Well, well," the storekeeper said aloud. "What did he want with a box of shotgun shells, buckshot at that?"

Miles Hinton stopped outside of town, transferred the shotgun shells to his saddlebag and studied the envelope. There was no return address. He tore the envelope open and drew out a single sheet of ruled white paper, unfolded it and read the large, careful handwriting.

"Dear Mr. Hinton

"I hope this reaches you in time. You said you would wait until the time seemed right to act so I'm hoping this letter will get to you before you start doing the job I hired you to do. I don't know what ever possessed me to hire a professional gun man, for if you did what

I asked you to I could never go back there to live any way. I should always be afraid the law would find out somehow that I was behind all the killin. So please disregard everthing I said and for God's sake don't kill anyone. You can keep the mony I already paid you for your trouble. Please do burn this letter as soon as you read it as I'd be worried about it if you didn't although I won't sign it. You know who I am any way."

There was a look of extreme distaste on Miles Hinton's normally expressionless face as he glanced back over what he had read. They're all alike, he thought. They hadn't got the guts to do their own killing, so they hire someone and then get cold feet about that. Well, Mr. Harris Thacker, maybe I should have told you, when I contract to do a job I always finish it—and then I'll be coming after the rest of my pay.

Hinton did one thing Thacker had requested—he took time to burn the letter before riding on. Not because it might get Thacker in trouble, but because it might get *him*, Miles Hinton, in trouble, if it was ever discovered in his possession or among his things. At the very least he would have a hard time explaining it, so he destroyed it with a sulphur match.

He rode on into the hills, keeping close enough to the 3-Bar road to spot any riders, but not close enough to be spotted except by very sharp eyes or pure chance.

The sun was already down and there was a chill in the air when he turned toward the Pollard shack and walked his horse through the rocks and cedars, being careful to leave as few tracks as possible on the hard ground. His eyes moved constantly as he rode, searching every bit of cover—yet he was no more than twenty feet from Bowdry when he first saw him.

The gunfighter was standing beside a cedar off to Hinton's right, blending in with the tree's dark shadow. He was turned sideways, making as little target as possible—and the twin barrels of the Greener rested in the crook of his left arm, pointed toward Hinton as if by accident. His right thumb rested lightly on the right hammer— also as if by accident. It was the way hunters often carried their guns, cradled comfortably in their arms yet ready for instant use.

Bowdry's face was like stone. His eyes were almost black in the fading light. He studied Hinton in silence for a time, the latter having halted at sight of him. Then Bowdry asked, "What's your game, friend?"

Hinton shook his head, watching the gunfighter carefully through his glassy gray eyes. "I'm not your friend and I don't know what you're talking about."

"I never thought you were my friend," Bowdry said, "but I know damn well you know what I'm talking about."

"Afraid not," Hinton said. "You'll have to tell me."

"I had a feeling I hadn't seen the last of you back at the hotel," Bowdry said. "Not after you took the trouble to go through my stuff without taking anything."

"I never went through your stuff. Someone else might have, but it wasn't me."

"It was you all right," Bowdry said. "It was also you who shot that white-haired fellow and two or three others."

"That's a pretty strong charge," Hinton said.

"I know it is," Bowdry agreed. "Don't misunderstand me. I don't care how many of that bunch you shoot. I figure they all need killing. But you're making it seem like I'm the one who's doing it all. That's what I don't like. If I ever get shot or hung, it's going to be for something I did, not for something you did."

Hinton glanced at the shotgun, wondering if he cold draw and fire before Bowdry could cock and squeeze. He decided it was unlikely, and in any case he needed Bowdry a while longer, needed him to take the blame. Killers who became known killers did not last very long—if the law did not get them, someone else did—and Miles Hinton intended to last long enough to retire with a hefty bankroll.

And as for the men Bowdry killed—well, Hinton intended to collect for those too.

No, he did not want Bowdry dead yet for a while. He was too valuable alive.

"You must have me mixed up with someone else," Hinton said. "I ride out this way pretty often, but I haven't shot anyone."

"There ain't much doubt in my mind about the ones I mentioned,"

Bowdry said. "I'm just wondering if you killed the old man too, so the Wadleys would be blamed for it. Or maybe you even thought I'd be blamed for it. I imagine a lot of people will think it was me."

"You've got quite an imagination," Hinton said. "You better watch it doesn't get you in any more trouble than you're already in. It appears to me you've already got enough enemies without going out of your way to make more."

"*Somebody* killed him," Bowdry insisted.

"I've got no argument with you there, but it wasn't me." Hinton lifted the reins. "I'm going to ride on now. If you mean to stop me, you'll have to shoot me in the back. But I don't think you're the type."

"You better keep in mind what I told you, friend," Bowdry said. "I don't want them bastards coming after me again because of something you did."

"And I told you you're not my friend," Hinton replied and put the sorrel in motion, heading directly toward the 3-Bar to show Bowdry he would do whatever he pleased. And as he rode on south into the deepening dusk, Hinton was more determined than ever that Bowdry should be blamed for whatever happened and suffer the consequences alone. Nobody told Miles Hinton what he could do and what he couldn't.

Before moonrise he tied his horse on the cedar hill overlooking the 3-Bar layout, got the shotgun from his blanket roll and loaded it with buckshot, slipping several more shells into his coat pockets. Then he squatted on his heels and studied the huddle of buildings in the valley below for some time. Lights glowed in both the main house and the bunkhouse and now and then a shadowy figure crossed between the two. Several times he heard voices raised in argument.

Rising, he made his way cautiously down the slope.

In the main house Rufe Wadley was staring, red-faced and angry, at Josh Larkin. "I ain't much interested in no more of yore bright ideas. It's a wonder Bowdry didn't kill Gord and Clete because of you. I'm just wonderin' why he never. I'd like to think on that a while before we do anything else."

"He was just playin' games, that was all," Larkin insisted. "Tryin' to make us look like fools.

"It wasn't all that hard to do," Rufe Wadley said, lighting a cigar from a box Harris Thacker had left behind. There were only a few left in the box and Rufe did not offer Larkin one. Gord Wadley lounged in a corner of the room, grinning stupidly, but smart enough not to ask for a cigar himself.

"I tell you what I got in mind this time will work," Josh Larkin said almost pleadingly, a look of near desperation in his eyes. Somehow he just had to get Lucy away from the Pollard place before anything happened between her and Bowdry. He had seen no sign of her or her pinto, but he supposed the pinto was wherever Bowdry kept his horses and that Lucy was hiding somewhere in the rocks— perhaps watching when Bowdry had made Gord and Clete scare him off with flying lead. Josh could picture her laughing at him and he ground his teeth in bitter rage at the thought. He would show her. He would show her and Bowdry too.

"It won't hurt to listen to him," Gord said, grinning.

"I already listened to him once," Rufe said, shaking the match out, "and it nearly got you killed."

"What I got in mind this time is so simple it's just shore to work," Larkin insisted. Rufe was puffing his cigar angrily and scowling at him through the smoke, but Josh didn't stop. He went on doggedly, the rest of this face seeming to hide behind his big white teeth. "Bowdry's only one man. He can't be ever'where at once and he can't watch ever'where at once, 'specially at night. Maybe we can't find him in the dark, like you said. But a few of yore boys could sneak through them rocks down to that old shack and wait in there till it's daylight. Then the first time Bowdry comes down out of them rocks, they can plug him. And sooner or later he'll have to come down to that waterhole atter some water."

"How do you know he won't be waitin' in that shack for them?" Rufe Wadley asked. "For all we know he may be sleepin' in there."

Larkin shook his head. "I tell you he stays up in them rocks. Ever' time I've been over there that's where he was."

Rufe Wadley smoked his cigar thoughtfully. "It might work," he said after a time. "I shore wouldn't mind gettin' possession of that old shack. And that waterhole even more so. But I'm beginnin' to wonder if it's worth the trouble and the price in blood Bowdry aims to make us pay. If he's willin' to let it stop here, like he claims, that would prob'ly be the smart thing to do. Much as I'd like to see him pay for all he's done."

Just then the window seemed to explode and flying glass and buckshot filled the room. Josh Larkin and Gord Wadley dived to the floor and Rufe Wadley fell over backward in his chair, almost swallowing his cigar and bellowing a hoarse cry of rage. "Sonofabitch! Git him you bastards! Don't let him git away!"

The three in the small room stayed down, but men began pouring from the bunkhouse, to be met at the door by another blast from the shotgun. They fell back inside, piling up on the floor, several of them stung by the pellets and all badly frightened. Someone got the door shut, someone else shot the light out, almost starting a fire. By the time Rufe Wadley's bellowing voice restored order, the man with the shotgun was long gone and no one knew which way he went.

"Son of a bitch!" Rufe Wadley roared, touching his cheek where glass or buckshot had drawn blood. "All right Larkin! We'll see if this new plan of yores is any better than the last one—and it damn shore better be!"

CHAPTER 13

It is not known when Bowdry slept. He must have slept sometime. Or what he ate, for he did not have a chance to do much cooking. But up in the rocks that night he must have got to thinking about the food Lucy Reardon had left in the shack. For he had started toward the shack when he saw three dark figures approaching it from the north ridge.

They were almost to the shack when he saw them, and he had just come out of the rocks near the waterhole. He levered several shots at them with the Henry as he backed into the rocks, but the three scrambled into the old shack unhit and returned his fire through the window whose glass had long since been shot out. They used their handguns, for Bowdry had taken the only two rifles among the entire outfit.

The three men in the shack were Gord Wadley, his cousin Zeb, and new a man, Barney Corvin. Another man had come with them to take back the horses. So it was that Gord, Zeb and Barney found themselves stranded, pinned down in the old shack. They had brought along both food and water to last several days, but in their excitement had let it go back on the horses. They had planned to shoot Bowdry when he came down to the waterhole, but unknown to them he had plenty of water in the natural tank which he had filled up in the rocks, and it was they who now had to figure a way to reach the waterhole before they died of thirst.

Come first light, they found the food Lucy Reardon had left and they devoured it like hungry wolves, chuckling at the thought that it had been left for Bowdry. But there was no water in the shack, and as the morning advanced and their thirst increased they stood at the window and gazed at the waterhole, only to be driven back by a well-placed shot or two from the Henry. They saw the puff of smoke up in the rocks but they did not see Bowdry.

Much to the annoyance of the other two, Gord Wadley kept grinning at their predicament.

Barney Corvin was a tall slouchy man with a pockmarked face and thick black brows. He watched Gord Wadley with a darkening scowl and finally grunted, "What the hell you grinnin' at? You crazy or somethin'?"

"Better to laugh than to cry," Gord said, waddling about the shack as if hunting a way out.

Zeb Wadley was—well, a Wadley, but taller than Gord and not as fat. "You're the one got us in this mess," he told his cousin. "It was yore idea. Yores and Rufe's."

"Hell no it wasn't neither," Gord said. "It was Josh Larkin's idea. He thunk it up all by hisself."

"Then I aim to cut his throat the next time I see him," Zeb said. "Now he's gone back to the LR where that redheaded woman's waitin' fur him, and we're stuck here without no water or grub, to say nothin' of wimmen."

"Hell, she may still be up there in them rocks with Bowdry," Gord said. "Josh said that's where she prob'ly was."

"He's crazy," Zeb said. "If Bowdry had him a woman, they would have been over there in that bed, and we'd be takin' turns by now our own selves."

Gord, who had a somewhat dirty turn of mind, chuckled at that.

"That's it," Barney Corvin said with a murderous scowl. "You two can laugh and tell jokes while we all starve and die of thirst."

"You don't know nothin' yit," Gord told him cheerfully. "You jist wait a few days."

"Hell, it looks like I'll have to wait," Corvin growled. "We stick our heads out that door he can pick us off—even at night."

In the end it was Gord Wadley who stood at the window, waved his hat and yelled, "Hey Bowdry! Don't shoot! It's me, Gord Wadley! How about lettin' us git some water! Then we'll leave!"

The answer was a jeering laugh from the rocks and a bullet that splintered his face. Gord jumped back with a grunt, tripped and sat down hard. He sat there with a stunned look, picking splinters out of his fuzzy cheek. It was not so much the shot that surprised him— he had half expected that. It was the mocking laugh. He had not thought of Bowdry as a man with a sense of humor.

Gord noticed the other two watching him with unsympathetic scowls. It was clear they blamed him for his failure, even though they had both said beforehand it would not work, Bowdry being the kind of man he was. Gord got awkwardly to his feet and dusted off his pants, saying with a sheepish grin, "I guess he don't aim to let us have no water or leave neither. He's prob'ly mad 'cause I come back over here."

Barney ground his teeth and turned away. Zeb, Gord's own cousin, a jolly companion in former times, stared at him with hatred.

And this was only the first day in the shack, a day not yet over.

Josh Larkin had spent the night at the 3-Bar, hoping for news in the morning that Bowdry was dead. But morning came and there was no news. Still none at noon. The three men had not returned from the old Pollard shack.

Larkin, though worried himself that something had gone wrong, tried to reassure his not very gracious host. "Bowdry prob'ly ain't come down for no water yit," he drawled. "Reckon he had his canteen full. But a canteen shore won't last him and two horses much longer."

Just then a red-bearded young man came in, his eyes shifty and clouded with dread. He was short and rather plump and vaguely resembled the rest of the Wadley clan. He was Cob Jensen, a cousin.

"What's on yore mind, Cob?" Rufe asked, his thick fingers impatiently drumming the desk behind which he sat like a bull with a red human face.

"I didn't tell you last night, Rufe," Cob said in an unsteady voice. "I knew you'd git mad. So I waited, hopin' they'd git back by now and it wouldn't matter. But seein' as how they ain't come back yit, I thought I better tell you."

"Tell me what?" Rufe bellowed, with a threatening scowl.

Cob flinched, passed a hand over his scared eyes, then took a deep breath and went on. "Well, I didn't even know about it till I got back and started unsaddlin' them horses, but them boys forgot about their water and that sack of grub."

Rufe glared a moment with a baffled look on his red face, as if knowing this was somehow bad but failing to divine its exact nature. Normally it would not have bothered him for his men—even his own brother—to go without food and water. They could always come back to the ranch if—then it hit him. This time, perhaps they could not come back. They were trapped in the Pollard shack without horses, without food or water.

His forehead seemed to retreat from his angry red eyes as he leaned forward over the desk. "Say that again!" he roared, then did not wait for Cob to repeat himself. He turned his withering gaze on Josh Larkin, who instinctively drew back a step, feeling behind him for the door. "You realize what this means? Them boys is over there without no food or water!"

"Nah," Josh said with a confidence he did not feel. "They's plenty of food and water in that old shack. Old man Pollard always kept the bucket full and plenty of grub on hand."

"Old man Pollard has been dead for close to a week!" Rufe snorted. "Bowdry's prob'ly et up most of the grub by now and got the rest up in them rocks with him! The water bucket too!"

"Nah," Josh said.

"Nah, hell!" Rufe exploded, heaving himself to his feet and pointing a stubby finger at Larkin. "You and yore bright ideas will get us all killed!"

Larkin backed toward the door, bumping into Cob, who was also on his way out. "Well, I b'lieve I'll go on home till you cool off," Josh said.

"You do that!" Rufe told him. "And don't come back over here with no more of yore crazy plans!"

On the way back to the LR, Larkin kept hoping Lucy had returned.

But when he saw old man Pollard's strawberry roan in the corral, it did not occur to him that Lucy might have ridden the horse home, for he knew nothing of her pinto's fate, had forgot all about the fall the animal had taken at the Pollard place. He figured Bowdry had come to settle accounts with him for trying to get the gunfighter killed. Bowdry was smart enough to know he had had a hand in that business yesterday. At least that was what Larkin feared.

He halted well out of pistol range. Then, remembering that Bowdry now had a rifle, he suddenly wheeled the Appaloosa and galloped back another hundred yards, turned again and sat watching the small unpainted house. It was a dreary, bleak-looking place between two barren gray hills. No wonder Lucy did not like it there and talked all the time about leaving.

"Bowdry!" he called. "It ain't like you think! I never had no hand in that!"

Lucy flung the door open and bawled angrily, "Bowdry ain't here! Quit making a fool of yourself!"

Josh Larkin rode on in cautiously, halted before the door and sat his saddle watching Lucy's angry red face. "Where's yore pinto?" he asked.

"Dead!" she said bitterly, her eyes suddenly cloudy and damp. "He broke a leg in that fall. It's a wonder I didn't break my neck."

Larkin turned his horse toward the nearby pole corral, stepped down and began unsaddling. "Now don't go blamin' me, Lucy," he said. "You never should of gone runnin' off over there like that."

"I will again when I take a notion," she told him, standing at the door with her fists clenched on her hips.

He looked around at her, his face red and quivering with anger. But he did not say anything until he could trust his voice. Then, rubbing the Appaloosa down with a handful of dead grass, he said, "I'm surprised you even came back."

"I wouldn't have," she said, "but Bowdry was afraid I'd get hurt."

Larkin crushed the grass in his hand and glared at her. "You know what you are?" he asked.

"I should," she said. "You've told me enough times."

"You ain't nothin' but a little whore," he said.

"Well, ain't that the reason you hang around here?" she retorted.

Larkin turned the Appaloosa into the corral, put the bars back up, then stood looking at the other horse. "Why don't you turn that roan loose and let him go back home?" he asked.

"I think I'll keep him," she said, "if Bowdry don't say nothing. I think Mr. Pollard would have wanted me to have him."

"Yeah, I reckon he would," Josh said maliciously. "Atter you hung around over there so much, and tuck him all them cakes and pies and such. That old man et better than I did." He gave her a hard look as he went toward the door. "I don't know what all else he done."

"And you won't ever know," Lucy said, backing away from the door as he came in. "You'll spend the rest of your life wondering about it, but you won't ever really know, will you?"

"No, I won't!" Larkin said, getting down on his hands and knees to look under the bed. " 'Cause I can't b'lieve a word you say!"

"What on earth are you looking for?" Lucy asked. "Do you think I've got a man under the bed? Bowdry maybe?"

"I'm lookin' for my rifle," he said. "You hid it here somewheres."

"I already told you a dozen times I don't know anything about your old rifle. You probably left it somewhere and forgot about it."

"Don't hand me that! You hid it 'cause you was afraid I'd stand up in them rocks and shoot that old man when he come out of the house."

"I wouldn't put it past you," she said. "What do you want with it now? You aiming to try to get Bowdry yourself?"

Josh Larkin looked at her with an insane glitter of jealousy and hatred in his eyes. "Maybe I can't keep you from goin' over there," he said. "But there soon won't be nobody over there for you to see. Then I aim to go over there some night and burn that old shack to the ground, so nobody else won't move in there."

CHAPTER 14

Bowdry didn't know how much time he had left. To live. To enjoy the little things and even, perhaps, dream of things that could never be. Things other people took for granted but which could never be part of a gunfighter's life.

It had turned cold, with a strong wind from the northwest picking up dust and blowing it across the rocky hills, obscuring distant landmarks in a gray haze. To the east the stunted cedars writhed and danced in the wailing wind, making it difficult to detect any other movement. In the bowl below him, the old shack creaked constantly, causing him to wonder if the three men were opening the door to make a break. He had a crick in his neck from turning his head, trying to watch in every direction at the same time, and his eyes were bloodshot from the dust and lack of sleep.

He was lying in a prone position behind a low rock at the very top of the east ridge, facing the shack, the old Henry ready for instant use, the shotgun within easy reach, the Smith & Wesson pistols where they usually were, but hidden by the long black coat he had put on because of the cold wind.

This was the morning of the second day that the three men had been in the shack. Close to thirty-six hours in all.

"Hey, Bowdry!"

It was Gord Wadley back at the window, sounding a little hoarse from yelling so much and also, no doubt, because his throat was dry.

Bowdry didn't answer because he didn't want them to know where he was, or how far away he was. Almost out of rifle range. Also because he had nothing to say to Gord Wadley, that fat young fool he had warned not to come back over here. Now he could not decide what to do about them.

"I got to have some water, Bowdry!" Gord yelled, the first of the three to break despite his initial optimism. "You kin shoot me if you want to, but I got to have some water! I'm gonna leave my gun in here and come out! Don't shoot, now!"

Bowdry swore softly as the short fat man opened the door and stepped out, grinning like a happy idiot despite the note of desperation in his cracked dry voice. He looked up at the rocks, then at the waterhole below them. He swallowed and licked his lips, rubbed his mouth with an unsteady hand. He started toward the waterhole, saying loudly, "Don't shoot, Bowdry! I just got to have me some water." They might have been little boys playing a game and Gord saying, "Time out now while I git me a drink."

He began to run like a thirst-crazed horse scenting water, bent on quenching his thirst even if it meant death.

In the shack, Zeb Wadley and Barney Corvin watched him through the window in round-eyed amazement.

"He'll git his fool head blowed off," Zeb said.

"Serve him right," Barney grunted. "I'm tired of hearin' that big fat mouth of his. And he's the one talked us into comin'."

Zeb nodded. "I feel the same way. He's my cousin, but I got me a good mind to put a round in his fat rump myself, if Bowdry don't. It just wouldn't be right for him to fill his gut with water and us not have none."

"It looks like he's gonna make it without even gettin' shot at," Barney said in surprise, as Gord fell in the waterhole like a man trying to drown himself, with only his rear end stuck up in the air. They could see him cupping great double handfuls to his face, bathing in it, and their own thirst became almost unbearable. It was pure torture to watch Gord wallow around in the water.

"Hell, let's try it," Zeb said suddenly. "If he made it, maybe we can too."

"Wait a minute," Barney said.

Gord had stopped splashing around in the water, had raised his dripping red face to peer toward the rocks.

Standing beside a big rock, out of sight of the shack, Bowdry leveled the Henry at Gord and said in a quiet, angry voice, "Quit wallowing around in that water, you filthy pig."

"Huh?" Gord said, his little eyes almost popping out of their sockets.

"Huh, hell," Bowdry said. "Get out of there and come over here."

Zeb and Barney could not see Bowdry or hear what he said. But they saw Gord rise from the waterhole, rear end first, like a young bull from a buffalo wallow, and walk over to the rocks with his hands in the air. He stepped from sight behind a rock, and Zeb and Barney exchanged a silent glance, agreeing without a word not to try for the waterhole themselves just then.

Behind the big rock, Gord stopped, grinning sheepishly at Bowdry, who stood frowning murderously at him. "What you want?" Gord asked, trying to brazen it out.

"What you want, hell," Bowdry said. "You're one stupid son of a bitch, did you know that?"

It did not bother Gord. Not even the cocked Henry seemed to bother him. Bowdry had let him get the water, hadn't he? If Bowdry meant to shoot him, he would have done it already. So Gord stood there grinning, his confidence restored, his spirits lifted by the water sloshing in his belly. He was wet and muddy and long unwashed, an affront to the eyes and nose, and looking down the barrel of a Henry from the wrong end—yet he stood there grinning as if he knew everything would be all right.

Bowdry's jaws clenched and unclenched. His bloodshot eyes burned like fire through an icy glaze. His voice was soft and deadly. "You came back over here hoping to put a bullet in me, after already trying it once the same day. Now here you are thinking I'll let you go again."

"I was hopin' you would," Gord admitted.

"And what about the next time?" Bowdry asked. "If you manage to get me, you'll be grinning about it. And if you fail, you'll be grinning about that too, thinking I'll let you go again."

"No, I ain't comin' back over here no more," Gord said. "I learnt my lesson this time."

"You better have." Bowdry jerked his head to the right. "Start walking."

He watched Gord edge around him, then followed the short fat man up the rough slope through the rocks. Gord almost fell several times, and was panting for breath long before they reached the top.

"Ain't you worried about your pals back there?" Bowdry asked.

"I guess they kin look after theirselves," Gord said, grinning. "I reckon it's ever' man fur hisself."

"Looks that way," Bowdry agreed.

They stopped at the top of the ridge, Bowdry breathing easily, Gord not so easily. "Two days without no chuck or water shore takes it out of a man," Gord said, grinning. "You wouldn't have a little somethin' to eat around here, would you?"

"I've got plenty to eat," Bowdry said. "But I ain't in the habit of feeding people who try to sneak up on me in the dark." Then he asked, "Did you tell that fat brother of yours what I said?"

Gord scratched the pale fuzz on his plump red cheek. "Yeah, I told him. He seemed to be thinkin' about it, but atter you snuck up and shot the winder out with that scattergun—"

"You've lost me," Bowdry said. "I didn't go anywhere near the place. It must have been that other fellow I mentioned. I saw him sneaking around about dark that day, after you and that other one left."

Gord looked away, not saying anything for once, not even grinning. It was clear he did not believe there was any "other fellow." There was just Bowdry, in his simple opinion.

Bowdry sighed. "I don't guess you fools will ever believe there is anyone else till you're looking down the barrel of his gun, and then it will be too late. He's not going to give you a chance to come back after him later."

"Why would anybody else want to kill us?" Gord asked.

Bowdry shrugged. "Maybe he's just a public-spirited fellow who thinks the country would be better off without you. I'm inclined to agree with him there. I just don't like the idea of you bastards coming after me every time he takes a notion to do the country a good turn. Me, I got no public spirit to speak of at all. If I did I wouldn't keep letting you go like this."

"I figgered it was 'cause you liked me," Gord said, with his infuriating grin.

Bowdry regarded him with hard eyes. "Don't think that grin will save you the next time. If you come back over here with some more of that bunch to get me, I'm going to feel like the biggest fool alive for letting you go. And it's going to make me so mad I'll do my best to get you even if I don't get anyone else."

Gord shrugged, looking uneasy in spite of his grin. "I ain't comin' back, even if Rufe wants me to. He kin send somebody else the next time."

"There better not be a next time," Bowdry told him. "Now start walking. If I ever see you around here again, I'll start shooting."

Gord's grin faded and his mouth fell open. "You mean I got to walk all that far on foot?"

"That's the way people usually walk."

"I thought you might let me have a horse," Gord said. "How about that sorrel you tuck? I mean just to ride home on?"

Bowdry shook his head. "I don't know anything about it. There ain't no sorrel around here, unless one of you brought it."

"You shore about that?" Gord asked in surprise, looking about at the huge rocks. "Where at do you keep yore horses?"

"In a safe place," Bowdry said, his eyes cold.

Gord dropped his glance, remembering how lucky he was just to be getting out of here with his life. It would not do to push his luck. "Well, if I got to walk I better git started," he said. "It'll take me half a day, weak as I am from not eatin' nothin'."

"You ain't got a thing to worry about," Bowdry assured him. "You could live on your fat for a year."

"Yeah, I was beginnin' to think I'd have to," Gord said, grinning back over his shoulder as he stumbled down the rocky slope.

"Don't come back," Bowdry reminded him.

"I ain't," Gord said. When he was at the foot of the slope, out of hearing, he added to himself, "Not till I git me a horse and a gun nohow, and a bit of grub in my belly."

He turned along the old trail down the narrow valley and soon found himself stumbling along the canyon rim in his high-heeled boots. Afraid he might slip and splatter on the rocks two hundred feet below, he was about to move further back from the rim when he heard a horse walking along behind him.

Looking around, he saw a tall young man on a blaze-faced sorrel. Both the man and the horse seemed familiar, but Gord did not place either immediately.

"Where did you come from?" he asked, grinning his surprise.

"Just rode over here for a look at the canyon," the man said casually, watching Gord through blank light gray eyes.

A tenderfoot, Gord thought in mild disgust. One of them tenderfoots that comes out here to look at the rocks and all like they never seen no real country before.

Yet there was something about the man that made him uneasy, and when he noticed the bone-handled Colt, be became even more uneasy. In spite of his nice clothes and well-groomed look, the man did not look much like a tenderfoot. And too, Gord kept thinking he had seen the fellow someplace before, perhaps in town. He still did not know most of the people in that little town, and some of them he had never even seen.

"Fur a minute there I tuck you fur a horse thief," Gord said, with a disarming grin. "That there sorrel looks just like one somebody stole from us, except yores has got a little bigger blaze and that front stockin' is on the wrong laig."

"I hadn't noticed."

"But I can see now that ain't it," Gord added. "Anyways, I'm purty shore I know who stole ourn. He claims it wasn't him, but I ain't no fool. It couldn't be nobody else."

"Got the goods on him, have you?" the familiar-looking stranger asked. He was now abreast Gord, taking up one side of the narrow trail, so that Gord had to move closer to the edge of the cliff. "Is that what you're doing now, looking for your horse?"

"Nah," Gord said. "I'm on my way home now. That's the 3-Bar

south of here. Bowdry wouldn't let me have no horse, so I had to walk."

"Bowdry?"

"Yeah. That's the feller I was tellin' you about. He's been causin' us a lot of trouble. Me and two more went over there to pay him back fur it, but we forgot our grub and water and he wouldn't let us have none. Them other two boys is still over there in that old shack, but Bowdry let me go." Gord grinned. "I think he sort of likes me."

"That's interesting," the stranger said, his horse moving a little closer to Gord. "You think he might let the others go?"

"I don't know," Gord said, his mind on the talk, not even noticing how close he was getting to the edge. "I shore hope so. Them boys sort of blames me 'cause they think I talked them into goin' over there with me."

The stranger glanced back over his shoulder. "I haven't heard any shots. But maybe we couldn't hear them this far."

"Yeah, we could too," Gord said. "It ain't fur back up there. I still got a long ways to go. I was gonna ast if you'd let me ride up behind you. That horse could carry us both real easy, and these boots is killin' me."

"Why, sure," the stranger said, reining the sorrel toward Gord and lifting one foot from the stirrup. Gord was too close already, and it was the wrong side to mount from, but that fool tenderfoot did not seem to know the difference.

Gord cried out in alarm as the shoulder of the horse stuck him, knocking him off balance. His eyes widened in horror when the stranger's foot came on up to his chest, rested there for a second and then shoved him backward. He instinctively grabbed at the polished boot but it was jerked back out of reach, and a moment later he felt himself falling through space and heard himself screaming like a woman. Somewhere at the back of his mind was the dim fleeting thought that Bowdry had been telling the truth all along—there was someone else, but Gord had not believed him until it was too late.

When a rocky canyon floor was coming up at you from two hundred feet below, it was too late for just about everything, even prayers.

CHAPTER 15

In the old Pollard shack, as it was called, Zeb and Barney checked their guns, making sure there was a sixth cartridge in the chamber normally left empty under the hammer. Each had brought along a spare revolver, thrust in the belt, and there on the floor was the gun and shell belt Gord had left behind. Zeb pulled the gun from the holster and found three spent cartridges in the cylinder.

"He fired them shots when we was runnin' for the shack," Zeb said in disgust. "All that time he only had two shells in his gun."

"He was nothin' but hot air," Barney agreed. Then he asked, "You think he talked Bowdry into lettin' him go again?"

"Hell, he must have," Zeb said, replacing the empties in Gord's gun. Actually the gun had belonged to the dead Pink Deeble, but Gord had taken possession of it after Bowdry took his. Gord had had to let the belt out to the last notch. "It's been way over a hour since we saw him go in them rocks with his paws up," Zeb added, "and we ain't heard no shots."

"Think we could get away with a stunt like that?" Barney asked.

The two solemn, haggard men exchanged a glance, and then Zeb said, "I doubt it. I learned a long time ago not to try to get away with the kind of stuff Gord got away with. He was always lucky like that. If I thought we'd make it, I'd say yes. But I figger Bowdry would let us get nearly to the waterhole and then open up on us. I think I'd rather try what we agreed on earlier—go out shootin', duck around behind the shack and keep it between us and the waterhole while we run like hell for them rocks on the west slope. He won't be expectin' us to go that way, thirsty as we are, or to try it in broad daylight. We may even catch the bastard nappin'."

"Anythin's better than this," Barney said. "I figgered them others would try to get us out of here before now. They must know we ain't got no water or nothin' to eat. I figgered Gil and Rex would try to sneak in and get Bowdry even if they had to come by theirselves. I know I wouldn't leave them in a fix like this without tryin' somethin'."

"Rufe's the one I blame," Zeb said. "He's the one in charge. But Rufe don't give a damn about nobody but hisself. He let on like he was all broke up when Hunk was killed, but that was mainly for show, just a lot of talk. He never shed no actual tears, and he won't shed none over us."

Barney did not say anything. He was standing to one side of the broken window, studying the rocks above the waterhole. There was a look of sick dread on his face, which was pale and drawn under the dark stubble.

When they were almost ready, Bowdry suddenly called from somewhere up in the rocks, they couldn't tell just where, "You two in the shack!"

He had been silent for so long that they were now startled by this unexpected yell, just when they were about to make their desperate try for freedom.

It was Zeb who answered in a loud cracked voice, "Yeah, whadda ya want?"

"Leave your guns in there and come on out!" Bowdry called back. "I've decided to let you go—this time! But I intend to kill anyone who comes back over here looking for trouble."

"You think it's a trick?" Corvin asked.

Zeb shrugged, combing his red beard with his fingers. "I don't think we got much choice. We can't last much longer without water, and if we go out shootin' he can pick us off easy with that Henry. I ain't sure where he is, but he's a lot closer than I figgered."

"Ask him why he's doin' it." Barney said quietly. "Ask him why he's lettin' us go. He knows we come over here to kill him."

Zeb had taken Barney's place near the glassless window, so his voice would carry better. His throat was so dry he had trouble speaking. "Why you doin' it, Bowdry?" he called. "Why you lettin' us go?"

After a moment Bowdry answered with some reluctance, "In case I was wrong about Hunk Wadley and those other two, this squares it as far as I'm concerned! I already let Gord go twice now when I should have killed him! I will the next time! That goes for you two, if you come back over here! If you think I'm bluffing, just try me!"

Zeb said to Barney, "I think he really does mean to let us go—just like he means to kill us if we come back over here."

"Then let's get the hell out of here and worry about that later," Barney said, already unbuckling his gunbelt.

"I hate like hell to leave all these guns here," Zeb said. "He'll soon have all the guns we've got, if this keeps up. And after laughin' at Gord and Clete when they come back without theirs, I'd be ashamed to go back without mine. I hate to go out there unarmed anyhow, just in case it is a trick. We don't know for sure that he even let Gord go. He may be layin' up there someplace in them rocks with his throat cut or his head caved in."

Barney frowned and started to shake his head, then thought for a moment and nodded. "We'll have to leave the belts and holsters behind, but maybe we can sneak out a gun under our shirts and a few shells in our pockets without him noticin'."

Zeb grinned as he took off his gunbelt, made reckless by the knowledge that life and freedom awaited him outside the shack, and not the chilling threat of sudden death as he had feared only a few minutes before. "Hell, maybe we can even turn the tables on the bastard. Get the drop on him and let him beg for his life a while before we fill him full of holes."

Barney's bloodshot eyes grew dreamy at the thought, but he said, "We'll have to be careful. He ain't lived this long by bein' easy to kill."

"It sure would be somethin', though, wouldn't' it?" Zeb said, as he slipped his gun under his waistband and pulled his shirt down over it.

"Yeah, it would," Barney agreed. "But be careful, or you'll get us both killed.”

When they were both ready, Zeb looked at Barney and Barney nodded. They moved toward the door but stopped near it, and Zeb called, “All right, Bowdry, we’re comin’ out! Don’t shoot!”

“Come ahead!” Bowdry replied.

They opened the door and stepped out cautiously, studying the rocks with narrowed eyes, half blinded by the bright light outside.

“Hold it there a minute,” Bowdry called, still unseen in the rocks, his exact location hard to determine. “I want you both to pull your coats and shirts up over your heads.”

The two exchanged a quick glance, then Zeb called, “What for?”

“So I can see what you’ve got under them.”

Zeb grinned tensely. “You mean you don’t trust us”

“No.”

Barney said out of the side of his mouth, “What we gonna do now?”

“Hell, I guess we’ll have to do like he says,” Zeb muttered. “I can’t even see him, but I bet he’s got that Henry aimed right at us and his finger on the trigger.”

“That old Henry shoots them old rimfire ca’tridges,” Barney said. “About how often you figger it misfires?”

“Not often enough,” Zeb said. “Now who’s gettin’ reckless?”

“It was just a thought.”

Up in the rocks, Bowdry asked, with an edge of impatience in his tone, “What are you boys waiting for?”

The two men seemed to sag, to wilt on their feet. Cussing softly, then pulled their coats and shirts up over their heads, so that their faces were hidden. But everything was hidden from them. They waited, like blindfolded and condemned men at a firing squad, tensed for the bullets that might come at any moment.

“That wasn’t very smart,” Bowdry said in a hard and taunting voice.

“You’d of done the same in our place,” Zeb replied through the coat and shirt.

“Maybe I would at that,” Bowdry said. “Turn around real slow. Now face me again and get rid of those guns. Or try to use them. It’s up to you. I'd just as soon kill you now as later. You boys don't ever learn."

They dropped the guns, then stood waiting.

"Now get out of here," Bowdry said harshly. "If you ever come back around here again, I swear I'll kill you both. That goes for the others. I'm at the end of my patience."

The two men, hard-faced and narrow-eyed, turned and went slowly toward the waterhole, still not speaking even to each other, and drank all they wanted, then deliberately washed their dirty bearded faces, although they knew Bowdry was watching them. It was an act of defiance and he would recognize it as such. But Bowdry remained silent and they took their time, for they felt certain he would not shoot them while they were unarmed. For that scruple they bore him no gratitude, only contempt, and already in the mind of each was the intention to come back with the others when they came after the gunfighter.

When they were done at the waterhole, they went up through the rocks and down the steep slope on the other side. It was only then that Zeb said, "I shore wish it'd been me up there with that Henry and him in my sights, instead of the other way around. I'd like to talk to him the way he talked to us, then fill the bastard full of lead."

"Me too," Barney Corvin said. Then he asked, "About how far is it to the ranch?"

"It's a lot farther on foot then it is on a horse," Zeb told him.

Barney sighed.

They turned along the old trail that led down the narrow valley, and Zeb soon said, "Looks like Gord come down this way. There's his boot tracks."

"Let's follow him," Barney said.

"Maybe he knows a shortcut."

"If there's a shortcut, you can bet Gord knows it," Zeb said.

They went on along the old trail, which at some point in the past had been used by wagons. There were two faint ruts separated by brush and weeds that overhung the ruts themselves and made the going difficult. On their right they saw where the steep ridge ended in a huge pile of rocks overlooking the head of the canyon. To the left were the cedar hills, spotted with rocks and brush, and cut by shadowy ravines. It seemed a rather scary place to two unarmed men on foot, who had just narrowly escaped death.

After a short silence Barney spoke in a low guarded tone, as if someone other than Zeb might hear him. "What Bowdry said about Hunk Wadley and them other two—I never did get the straight of that. What happened?"

Zeb shrugged, and kept his own voice low. "Rufe sent them over to get Bowdry. But he got them instead."

Barney glanced aside at the red-bearded man. "All three of them?"

Zeb nodded. "I guess he took them by surprise. Saw them comin' and was waitin', I guess. Same thing happened when Moose Grogan and them Mexicans went after him."

"I heard about that," Barney said. He was about to add something, when he happened to glance at the ground and stopped dead in his tracks. "Hey, look at this. Somebody come down this way on a horse not too long ago. Here's another track—and this one's on top of one of Gord's boot tracks. Looks like he was following Gord." Barney shot Zeb a quick look. "You think it was Bowdry?"

Zeb was studying the ground with worried eyes. But after a moment he said, "How could it be Bowdry? He's still up there in them rocks."

"Yeah, but we don't know how long he'd been up there," Barney said. "We never heard nothin' out of him for way over a hour after Gord left."

"That's right," Zeb admitted, looking off down the trail. "I got me a feelin' I don't like. Let's foller them tracks a piece and see what we find."

The ground was hard and rocky along the canyon rim and there were few tracks. But they kept to the old wagon road and soon found where the ground had been badly scuffed by both horse and boot tracks. It looked to them as if Gord and the horse walking along beside him had tried to push each other off the road and Gord, being somewhat smaller, had got the worst of it.

Zeb and Barney stepped over to the rim and peered down into the canyon below.

"Does that look to you like Gord layin' on them rocks down there?" Zeb asked.

Barney nodded. "What's left of him." They stared in grim silence for a time, and then he added, "Looks like he found hisself a shortcut to the bottom of that canyon in a hurry."

"With somebody's help he did," Zeb said, and then he did, what was for him, a very unusual thing—he crossed himself, a dark gesture he had often seen border Mexicans make to ward off evil. "Let's get back away from this canyon. I've follered old Gord as far as I aim to in that direction."

They crossed the road and climbed into the rocks and cedars on the other side, stumbling in their haste, their legs shaky from weakness and fear. Zeb, the heavier man, kept in the lead with difficulty, Barney so close behind that he had to keep his arms up to protect his face from swinging limbs.

"You think he'll come after us?" Barney asked.

"What the hell kind of game does he think he's playin'?" Zeb said resentfully. "That ain't the first time he's pulled a stunt like that. He let Gord and Clete go the other day, then snuck up to the 3-Bar that very night and shot through the winder with a shotgun. I guess he was tryin' to kill Gord then. And before you come here he killed Pink Deeble—right after lettin' on like he didn't want no more trouble."

"Yeah, I heard about that," Barney said "I was thinkin', Zeb—if he is after us, maybe we better hole up someplace till dark."

"I'd rather get as far away from here as we can," Zeb said, casting a wild look at the nearby rocks. "This place gives me the creeps."

"I'd feel a lot better if I had a gun," Barney said.

He suddenly stopped, putting a hand on Zeb's shoulder to stop him. "Listen," he said softly.

Zeb looked around at him with that wild, scared look in his eyes. "What is it?"

"Thought I heard somthin'."

There were in a narrow, V-shaped ravine between two rocky slopes covered with low cedars. There were rocks and cedars in the ravine itself, and thick gray brush in places. They could not see much over fifty feet in any direction.

"What did it sound like?" Zeb whispered.

"I ain't sure," Barney said. "The first time I heard it I just thought it was the noise we was makin'. Then I heard it again—sounded like a horse or somethin' walkin' on rocks. But when we stopped it did too, whatever it was."

"Where did it sound like it was comin' from?" Zeb asked.

"I couldn't tell. We were makin' too much noise. And I ain't never been much good at tellin' where sounds was comin' from."

"Hell, I ain't neither," Zeb said. "I never did figger out just where Bowdry was back there when he was talkin' to us."

"Same here."

They were silent for a minute, and then Zeb said in a low voice, "You know somethin'? I'm beginnin' to wish we was back in that old shack. At least we had our guns and plenty of shells."

"Listen!" Barney hissed, again grabbing Zeb's arm to silence him.

"I heard it that time," Zeb whispered. "Sounded like a horse stepped on a rock. Let's get the hell out of here."

"Wait, Zeb! He'll hear us if we move."

"Hell, he knows where we're at anyway," Zeb said. "He's just tryin' to sneak up on us. Next thing, he'll leave that horse behind and we won't be able to hear him, no more than we could hear him movin' around up in them rocks."

"We've got to find a place to hide," Barney insisted. "When it gets dark maybe we can make it to the ranch. But we won't never get there in the daylight without him spottin' us."

"I know a place over by the road to the ranch," Zeb said. "If they come lookin' for us, that's the way they'll come, and I'd sure hate to miss them."

"How far is it?"

"Hell, it can't be far. That road ain't much over half a mile from the canyon, and we've already come a pretty good piece."

"All right," Barney decided. "But let's take off our boots so he won't hear us, and step where we won't leave no tracks."

"I ain't got no socks," Zeb protested. "We'll ruin our feet."

"Better our feet than us," Barney said.

Miles Hinton had dismounted and was leading his horse. He could have moved more quietly without the horse, but he did not know just where the two men were. There was a chance they had already spotted him, might even now be watching him, and not shooting only because they had nothing to shoot with. If he tied the horse and continued his stalk without it, they might circle around behind him, pile on the sorrel and hightail it for the 3-Bar, leaving him afoot and in bad trouble. For the horse could easily be traced to him.

But he did not think they had seen him, and he was hoping they wouldn't until he had them in his sights. In case they managed to get away, he did not want them to know who he was. He wanted them to think it was Bowdry stalking them. That was why he was being so careful, covering his own tracks while he tried to follow theirs.

He had not heard them moving for quite a while now, but that did not mean they were still stopped. He figured they had taken off their boots and slipped on up the ravine toward the 3-Bar road. But if they were as cautious and clever as they seemed, they would hide out in the brush and rocks near the road and wait until night before going on to the ranch, knowing—as they obviously did—that they were being followed.

Hinton tucked the Ethan Allen shotgun under his arm and looked at his gold pocket watch. Not quite two o'clock. Still several hours of sun left, and even longer till full dark. He had thought about circling ahead and waiting by the road for the two men, but too much could happen between now and nightfall, and they might even avoid the road as the most likely spot for an ambush.

After listening for a time and hearing only the wind in the cedars, Hinton led his horse on up the ravine, searching for tracks. He finally found one—the track of a bare human foot—in a little patch of sand. He studied it with a cold gleam of satisfaction in his pale eyes. So he had guessed right. They had removed their boots. That explained why he had not heard them move on after stopping back down there. And it appeared that they meant to follow the twisting ravine on up to the 3-Bar road. Perhaps they were afraid that if they climbed out of it he would spot them on the rocky slope where the cedars were too stunted and scattered to provide much cover.

Hinton was tired of walking and his feet were beginning to hurt.

He got back on his horse and rode on up the ravine at a walk, the shotgun across the pommel. The ravine forked ahead and he turned up the left fork—although he felt certain the two men had taken the right as it would take them a little closer to the 3-Bar.

Up here both forks were getting shallow and the ridges on either side lower, the ground leveling off, but broken by knolls covered with rocks and brush. Hinton felt certain the two men would be hiding on one of these mounds of rock and brush where they could watch the road to the ranch—and watch for him at the same time.

He crossed the road openly, then began working his way south, methodically searching every possible hiding place. If he flushed them from their cover, as he hoped to do, it would be only a matter of minutes before he rode them down.

It happened sooner than he had expected. As he was about to leave one of these low brushy hills where a few trees grew among the rocks, he saw them running away from the one just ahead of him, angling down toward the 3-Bar road. They ran very awkwardly in their high-heeled boots, which they had put back on, and one of them—the fat one—stumbled and fell just as they reached the road.

Miles Hinton bared his teeth in a wolfish grin as he broke the shotgun open to check the loads. He closed the breech and was already leaning forward in the saddle to begin the chase, when he saw a cloud of dust approaching from the south. Only moments later nine men rode up and halted beside the pair on foot, who began talking excitedly and turning to point toward the brushy knoll where Miles Hinton sat his horse.

CHAPTER 16

Miles Hinton's first thought was to turn and ride for it. But he checked the impulse. Harris Thacker had owned some very good horses, known for their speed and stamina, and most, if not all of them, had fallen into the hands of the Wadley gang. The bright red chestnut Rufe Wadley now rode had been Thacker's personal mount and was considered the fastest horse in this part of the country, even faster than Josh Larkin's Appaloosa. Some of the other 3-Bar horses were said to be almost as fast.

Hinton knew they had seen him, but he did not think they could see him clearly because of the brush and trees. He eased the shotgun down on the off side of the horse and let it drop in some tall dead weeds. He could come back for the shotgun later—if they did not find it first.

Then he rode down the slope toward the 3-Bar men, waving casually as he approached.

Rufe gaped in baffled rage at the unadulterated gall of a man he meant to kill. Then he suddenly leaned forward in his saddle to peer at the approaching rider, and raised his arm to stop his trigger-happy bunch from using the guns they had drawn. "Hold it," he barked. "That ain't Bowdry."

"Then what in hell was he doin' up there?" Zeb asked, his narrow bloodshot eyes darting looks of pure murder at the rider. "And what's he doin' on that sorrel Bowdry took?"

Rufe snorted. "You've got the wrong horse and the wrong man. That's that dude from the hotel in town. He rides out this way and shoots at rocks and trees with that purty gun of his. Tryin' to make-believe he's a cowboy, I guess."

He turned to Hinton as the latter rode up and halted. "You have any idea how close you come to gettin' shot, ridin' around here on a horse like that?" Rufe asked angrily, for he had no time to waste on stupid greenhorns when he had a man like Bowdry to hunt down. "That horse looks almost exactly like one Bowdry stole from us. When them two there saw you they thought it was Bowdry, and if he hadn't took their guns, they would of blowed yore fool head off."

Hinton glanced casually at Zeb and Barney, and in his round gray eyes there was a look of mild contempt—all the more galling because they considered him a wet-eared dude who should not even be trying to ride a horse, much less wearing a gun. "I saw them run off down the hill there," he said quietly. "I was ready to light out myself, because I figured they must have seen a bunch of wild Indians."

A few of the men guffawed and others grinned at the red-faced pair standing there, still out of breath, in the clothes they had torn running through the brush.

"What were you doin' back there in that bresh?" Zeb asked, still hard-eyed and suspicious.

"Hunting rabbits," Hinton said easily.

"Huntin' rabbits!" Zeb echoed. "With a handgun?"

Hinton nodded innocently. "I've never hit one," he admitted. "They run too fast."

There was more coarse laughter from the mounted 3-Bar men, and Zeb's face got that much redder. Barney, calmer and quieter, stood a little to one side, watching Hinton carefully out of the corners of his eyes—eyes still haunted by the cold dread that had crept over him while they were fleeing from this dude they had thought was Bowdry.

"You better hunt rabbits someplace else from now on," Rufe told Hinton. "Ain't you heard there's a war goin' on around here?"

"I heard some talk about it in town," Hinton said. "Tell you the truth, I rode out this way hoping to see some of it. That's the reason I sort of followed along after those two. I figgered sooner or later they'd run into Bowdry and I'd get to see a good shootout."

"I knowed it!" Zeb said. "I knowed all along somebody was follerin' us!"

Rufe glanced at him in disgust. "Bowdry chasin' you," he sneered. "Looks like you boys got spooked by a dude." Then he gestured impatiently at Hinton. "Go on, get outta here, before somebody takes a shot at you."

"Well, all right," Hinton said, reluctantly turning the sorrel around. "I didn't mean to cause no trouble. I only wanted to watch."

"Damn fool," Rufe grunted, as he watched the dapper young man ride off. He bit off the end of a cigar and looked at Zeb. "Where's Gord? He still over there?"

"That's what we been tryin' to tell you!" Zeb exclaimed. "Gord's dead! He's layin' down there on them rocks at the bottom of that canyon, waitin' for the buzzards. Maybe Bowdry never follered us, but he shore as hell follered Gord. Follered him and crowded him over the edge."

Rufe's mouth fell open and the cigar almost dropped out. Then, with a look of choked rage and grief on his face, he began to chew on the unlit cigar. "Show me," he said hoarsely, already turning the red horse toward the canyon.

A short time later Rufe stood on the canyon rim, peering down at the rocks two hundred feet below. "That's Gord all right. That's the old shirt he was wearin'. One he always wore. I'll be damned."

The others had also dismounted to line up along the rim and gaze in wonder at the vaguely human object far below.

"You can still see the tracks there where Bowdry's horse forced him over," Zeb said. "Must of rammed him purty hard to send him off the edge."

Rufe was still chewing on his cigar. Now he fired it up and puffed in angry silence for a time, still staring down at the smashed body of his dead brother.

Then he said, "One of you men go get Josh. This was his idea. We're goin' after Bowdry and he's gonna lead the attack. If anybody gets killed, I aim for him to get it first."

Miles Hinton followed the 3-Bar road toward town for nearly a mile, then turned off the road and circled back to the place where he had left the shotgun. The Wadley men were gone by then. He broke the shotgun down into two pieces and wrapped it carefully in his blanket roll. He was tying the blanket roll back on behind his saddle when he saw a horse and rider come out of the trees on the other side of the road and turn along it in the direction of town.

Hinton drew back into the brush and trees on the knoll and watched the rider go by, unaware of his presence. Then he mounted up, circled again through the cedars and angled down toward the road to intercept the rider.

Hinton had seen the shaggy-haired man several times in town and had learned his name was Corky Brill, a distant relative of the Wadleys. Corky had a sneering sunburnt face and a high opinion of himself. To judge by the look of contempt in his eyes, he did not have a very high opinion of Miles Hinton, the duded-up young man loping down to meet him. Actually, Hinton was as old or perhaps a little older than Corky, but seemed younger to Brill, who thought of all dudes as being young and inexperienced, and himself as being seasoned and experienced far beyond his years.

"You still foolin' around here?" Brill asked in a rude, arrogant tone. "I thought Rufe told you to git."

Uninvited, Miles fell in beside Brill and trotted along in silence a little distance. Then he said casually, his eyes on the road ahead, "Thought I saw a fox back there. I tried to follow it, hoping to get a shot, but it disappeared in some rocks and I couldn't find it again."

"Prob'ly a coyote," Corky said. He gave Hinton a look of pure scorn. "Where the hell you from anyway, that you can't even tell a fox from a coyote?"

Miles looked embarrassed at his ignorance. "Back East," he said, then quickly changed the subject. "Did you fellows ever find Bowdry?"

"Hell no," Brill said. "We ain't tried yet. But we found Gord Wadley at the bottom of that canyon back down yonder. Looked like Bowdry rode up beside him on his horse and crowded him off."

"You mean Bowdry did that?" Hinton asked in surprise. "He won't make many friends that way, will he?"

"He shore as hell won't," Corky agreed, grinning as if he found this big-eyed dude very amusing.

"I guess you're on your way to town to get the undertaker?" Hinton asked.

"Undertaker!" Corky exclaimed, as if he'd never heard of such a thing. "Heck, no! We don't bother with no undertaker out here. We got no time for fussin' over the dead. We just try to git them in the ground 'fore they git too ripe, then we go atter the bastards what killed 'em. No, I ain't goin' to town. I'm goin' atter Josh Larkin. It was his idea that got Gord killed, and Rufe aims for him to be with us when we go atter Bowdry."

"I'd sure hate to be in Bowdry's shoes," Hinton said. "Do you think Mr. Wadley would mind if I went along and watched?"

"You'd just git in the way," Corky said, grinning. "Or git yore fool head blowed off. Now you better dust on back to town, 'fore I take a notion to let some daylight through you."

"I know you're only joking," Miles said innocently. "But just out of curiosity, how would you go about it? It will only take a minute to show me."

Corky shrugged and reined in, still grinning, willing to indulge the greenhorn, who rode off a little to one side and turned his horse to face him, watching expectantly with his big bright eyes.

"Right here's how I'd go about it," Corky said, as his hand streaked toward his gun.

His fingers had barely touched the butt when he suddenly froze, blinking in wonder at the cocked gun in Hinton's hand. He had not seen the dude draw, had not seen him move.

"And this is how I'd go about it," Miles said, and blew a big red hole through Corky Brill's heart.

Bowdry and the Wadley bunch heard the shot at approximately the same time, being about the same distance away, though in different places. Both parties decided to investigate, but as Bowdry had to saddle his horse, the others arrived on the scene before him.

Tying his horse in some rocks near the road, he peered through the wind-blown cedars at Rufe standing over the dead man, chewing the stub of a dead cigar. The others were nearby, some on the ground and some still mounted.

"I'll be damned," Rufe said. "Two dead in one day."

"I knowed all the time Bowdry was around someplace!" Zeb said. "I bet he was watchin' us when we were talkin' to that dude! Hell, he may still be around here someplace!" The red-bearded man swept the area with a sharp glance, seeming to look directly at Bowdry.

Rufe was still chewing his cigar and gazing at the body of Corky Brill. He spoke as if to himself. "I aim to see that son of a bitch dead if it's the last thing I ever do."

Bowdry did not need anyone to tell him who "that son of a bitch" was. He quietly loosened the reins and led the brown horse away down through the cedars tossing in the cold wind, keeping the rocks between himself and the Wadley men.

The shot was completely unexpected. He had thought they were all back there on the road, crowded around the dead man. But evidently one of them had decided to scout around, or had been told to do so. It was the pale-haired Clete Anson, peering over a rock with a wild glitter in his green eyes and yelling, "There he goes! It's Bowdry!"

Bowdry cussed softly and bitterly as he swung astride the gelding and raced away, bent low to make as small a target as possible. They would never believe now that he had had no part in the killing. His presence in the area so soon afterward would finish convicting him in their minds, if they had ever entertained any doubt. They would never suspect the real murderer, Miles Hinton, a man who, for some reason, seemed to have it in for Bowdry almost as much as he did for the Wadleys.

And Bowdry, for his part, was coming to hate the man more than he had ever hated the Wadleys and their kin, even when he thought they had killed old man Pollard.

Clete Anson, a man whose life Bowdry had spared, showed his gratitude by blazing away until his long-barreled pistol clicked empty, then began yelling excitedly for the others to go after the son of a bitch.

They were about to do just that, those on the ground leaping back into their saddles, when to their surprise Rufe began yelling at them to stay the hell where they were.

"Come back here you fools!" he roared. "I'm still general of this here army, and a damn good thing! You'll never catch up to him now before he gets back in them rocks, and he'll pick half of you off with that Henry when you charge the ridge!"

Clete Anson ran up yelling hoarsely, "Why didn't y'all go after him? I hit his horse! I saw it stumble! You could of caught him easy!"

Some of the men groaned at the missed opportunity, and one of them said, "Maybe we can still catch him. That horse may go a little piece and drop dead. I've seen it happen before."

"I'm still givin' the orders around here!" Rufe barked. "That horse prob'ly stumbled on a rock or somethin'. But it don't matter, 'cause I've made up my mind that Josh Larkin is gonna be the next man who gets shot goin' after Bowdry. He ain't gonna get my brother killed with his stupid ideas and then go back home and forget all about it. Cob, you and Rex go on to the LR and bring that bastard back with you if you have to tie him on his horse. But circle around where Bowdry won't see you go by. I can't afford to lose no more men."

Bowdry was almost back to the boulder-strewn ridge overlooking the old Pollard shack when the horse suddenly caved in under him. One moment the gelding was running strongly. The next he simply died on his feet. Bowdry's feet left the stirrups and he left the saddle, leaping clear with the Henry. He hit the ground, rolled to break his fall, and jacked a cartridge into the chamber of the Henry as he got to his feet. Then, seeing that the horse was already dead, he turned his attention to what was behind him. But apparently they had decided not to follow him, taking it for granted that with his head start he would make it back to the rocks before they could overtake him. They must not have known about the horse.

Bowdry, however, was a man who took nothing for granted. They might still decide to come after him. Wasting no time, he stripped the gear from the dead horse and lugged it up the steep ridge to his cache among the rocks. Then, taking both the rifle and the shotgun, he headed for his lookout on the crest, to watch for the 3-Bar men and wonder why they did not come.

Now for the first time he was really worried, not just in his mind but in his gut. Without a horse he felt like a man without any legs. He had never intended to leave until he was ready, but now he could not leave, not even to go after supplies, which he badly needed. They had immobilized him. They had him trapped.

CHAPTER 17

Cob Jensen did not relish the task before him. He wished Rufe had sent someone else in his place. He did not care for Rex Medlin's company. Rex was one of the new men and Cob was uneasy around him. Everything Rex said made him still more uneasy. He was afraid Rex would get them both killed. For Josh Larkin was known to have an unpredictable temper and to be mighty fast with those white-handled guns he wore.

Rex was the youngest of the three new men still alive, the loudest and by far the most reckless. He was a long-legged, long-armed young man with stringy blond hair and a big Adam's apple. He wore his gun low and stared at everything and everyone with truculent scorn in his hard brown eyes. Like some reckless and now dead men before him, he had boasted that he could go after Bowdry by himself. Bowdry, he had said, would stand no chance against him.

Now he was talking about Josh Larkin in the same vein.

"How much farther is it?" Rex asked.

"I ain't shore," Cob said.

"What do you mean you ain't shore?" Rex asked. "You don't even know the way over there, do you?"

"We keep ridin' southwest, we're shore to cut a trail sooner or later."

"What trail?" Rex snapped.

Cob tugged at his hat and studied the bleak gray country ahead with worried eyes. There were rocks everywhere, brush along the valley and stunted cedars on the hills, but not much grass anywhere. And he saw no stock, neither cattle nor horses.

"I figgered they'd have them a trail made to that old Pollard shack, they go over there so much," he said. "Or that woman does, and he goes over there to bring her back."

"Maybe there ain't no trail," Rex said, watching Cob with a growing anger. "They prob'ly don't go the same way enough to make one. If you didn't know the way over there, you should of told Rufe so he could send somebody else."

"I wish he had," Cob said.

"You scared?" Rex asked scornfully.

"Why would I be scared?" Cob asked, flushing with anger. "Ain't I got you along?"

"A good thing too," Rex said. "Don't you worry none. If there's any trouble I can handle it. You just keep out of the way."

"There ain't gonna be no trouble," Cob said, " 'cause we just gonna tell him what Rufe said."

"Like hell! You heard what he said. He said for us to bring that bastard back if we have to tie him on his horse."

"Rufe don't always say exactly what he means," Cob said. "I know he never meant for us to pick a fight with Josh. That wouldn't serve no purpose. Rufe don't want him dead, and he don't want us to get killed neither."

"You talk like he could get us both," Rex sneered.

"They say he's real fast," Cob said worriedly. "Maybe even as fast as Bowdry." Then he said, "There they are, Josh and that woman, Lucy Reardon. Looks like she's still ridin' old man Pollard's strawberry roan. That ain't a bad lookin' horse."

"That ain't a bad lookin' woman neither!" Rex said excitedly.

"Better not even look at her," Cob said. "He's crazy jealous."

"That's his hard luck," Rex said. "If he don't want nobody lookin' at his girl he should get him one that ain't worth lookin' at."

When they got closer, Cob, following his own advice, avoided looking directly at the red-haired, full-breasted young woman on the red-speckled horse with the red mane and tail. But he was very much aware of her presence even though he kept his eyes carefully on Josh Larkin. The big rustler showed a toothy grin but watched them with sharp, suspicious eyes to see if they paid too much attention to Lucy.

"What brings you boys over this way?" Larkin asked.

Cob shifted uncomfortably in his saddle. "It's sort of a long story."

"No, it ain't neither," Rex said. "Rufe sent us over here to get you."

Larkin cut his bright blue eyes at the gangling youth. "What's he want?"

"We're goin' after Bowdry and he wants you with us," Rex said maliciously, enjoying the look of uneasiness that came to Larkin's face. "His brother's dead and he figgers it was your fault."

"You mean old Gord's dead?" Larkin asked in his unexcitable drawl, though his face registered a minute shock. "How did it happen?"

"Bowdry pushed him off in that canyon over there," Rex said with obvious satisfaction.

"That's how it looks anyhow," Cob added. "Not long after that he killed Corky Brill, who was on his way over here to tell you. When we got there Clete Anson looked around and found Bowdry off below the road in some rocks, watchin' us. He got away, but Clete said he hit his horse. So Bowdry may be afoot now."

Cob was aware of Lucy watching him silently, but he kept his eyes on Larkin.

"You mean he ain't got no horse?" Josh asked. "What about that sorrel they said he tuck?"

"I ain't ever been so shore he stole that sorrel," Cob said. "When we went lookin' for them horses, I never saw no tracks leadin' toward that old shack."

"Who else could of done it?" Larkin asked. Then he suddenly flashed his big teeth in a grin. "You don't think it was me, do you?"

"Oh, no," Cob said quickly. "I never thought about it bein' you."

"We're wastin' time," Rex said. He nodded curtly at Larkin. "Let's go."

"Now hold on a minute," Larkin said. "That ain't my fight. Lucy wants me to stay out of it and I promised her I would."

"Like hell!" Rex cried, red-faced with anger. "It's too late for that now! You got Gord killed with yore big plan that didn't work! When you realized it hadn't worked, you thought you could just go on back home and forget about it! Well, it don't work that way, mister! Rufe said for us to bring you back and that's just what I aim to do! I don't want no argument neither!"

Josh gaped at the sputtering youth in astonishment, surprised at this unexpected display of rage and indignation. He had assumed the two were just delivering a message and had no personal feelings in the matter. When he got over his shock, his own face reddened and his voice shook a little with anger. "Don't you sass me, boy. You ain't even dry behind the ears."

Rex went rigid and his hand tensed like a claw near his gun. "Try me!" he cried.

Again Larkin gaped at the angry boy, taken aback by the threat of sudden violence, which he had not expected and was not prepared for. He was obviously a little shaken, and it seemed to Cob that he was backing down when he said, "I ain't gonna draw on no wet-eared boy. I'd just have Rufe and them atter me."

"No, you wouldn't neither!" Rex told him. " 'Cause you'd be dead!"

"You shore as hell couldn't do it," Josh snorted. "I just don't want to git up no trouble with Rufe and them. If it wasn't for that, I'd show you a thang or two."

"You're just backin' down and you know it." Rex said, suddenly calm again, but hard and merciless in his youthful scorn. He added the final insult. "You're yellow."

That reared Josh up in his saddle. "Who's yaller?" he asked.

"You are," the boy said, still quiet, for he seemed convinced now that Larkin did not have the guts to fight him.

"We'll see about that," Larkin said. "When we git over there I'm just liable to ask Rufe if it's all right with him if I call you out on that."

"Suits me," Rex said, content to wait.

Josh turned in his saddle and looked at Lucy Reardon, who was watching him intently. He had trouble meeting her eyes. "I reckon I better go on over there and see what Rufe wants," he told her.

"You know what he wants," she said. "They already told you what he wants."

"If I don't go I'll have to kill this young punk here," Josh said.

"Then kill him," she said.

The three men all looked at her in surprise. She seemed entirely calm and ignored the other two, keeping here eyes on Larkin. His chapped lips pulled together over his big teeth in an expression of bitter resentment. "And what if he got lucky and killed me?" he asked. "You wouldn't mind that too much neither, would you?"

"If you go over there," she said, "don't come back."

"Dammit, I got to go," he said, his voice rising in anger. "I ain't scared of that wet-eared punk, but if I kill him Rufe and them will be atter me like they're atter Bowdry. Is that what you want?"

"It would serve you right," she said, as merciless as the hard and scornful boy, Rex. "You never should of got mixed up in that. I tried to get you to keep out of it."

"Dammit, Lucy, you know why I got mixed up in it!" Larkin said, losing control of his temper. "It was yore fault. You kept runnin' over there to that old shack. I was out of my head with jealousy. You said so yoreself."

"You're still out of your head with jealousy," she said. "I saw how your face lit up when you saw them two coming. You were hoping for news Bowdry was dead."

"You shouldn't blame me," Larkin said bitterly. "You'll be runnin' back over there the first chance you git."

"I agreed to stay away from over there as long as you stay away from over there—and away from that Wadley trash," she said.

Cob, a second cousin of the Wadleys, hung his head in shame. For he knew she was right. They were all trash. Rufe, although he had been putting on airs lately and acting like a cattle baron on his stolen spread, was at the top of the heap. But Cob knew he too was trash, not as bad as the others only because he did not have the guts to be.

Josh was staring at Lucy with a puzzled frown. "Why you tryin' so hard to protect Bowdry anyhow? What's he mean to you, a stranger and all?"

"He don't mean anything to me," she said. "And I mean even less to him. I just don't want you making any bigger fool out of yourself than you already are."

"I'm a purty big'un, all right," Larkin admitted with poor grace. "If I wasn't, I never would of got mixed up with you."

She shrugged indifferently. "You can leave anytime. Just don't come back."

"I'll be back," he said. "And you better be there."

"We'll see," she said.

"Now dammit, don't go back over there where Bowdry is!" Josh said in a rising tone. "You tryin' to git yore fool self killed? They'll be comin' atter him any time."

"And you'll be with them, won't you?" she asked, watching him with her intent eyes.

"With us, hell!" Rex said, with a snort of scornful laughter. "He'll be leadin' us! Rufe aims to put him up front where he'll be the first man shot."

"We'll see about that," Josh said. "I'll ride over there and talk to him, but I ain't decidin' nothin' till I hear what his plan is."

"His plan is simple, not like yores," the kid grinned. "He aims to attack and he aims for you to lead the attack."

Arriving at the 3-Bar, Josh left his horse outside and tramped into the house where he had never set foot in Harris Thacker's time. A known horse thief and cattle rustler who preyed on Thacker's stock, he had not been invited, despite his friendly overtures. He had seen no reason why he and Harris could not be friends, being neighbors and all, but the rancher had thought otherwise. Now Larkin was here at the new owner's request—but the invitation had not been very friendly.

Rufe was enthroned behind the office desk, from which he seemed to think a cattle king should rule his empire. He was smoking the last of the cigars left behind by the former ruler. He did not rise and he did not ask Josh to sit. He sat there puffing his cigar as if trying to decide whether the horse thief should be shot or hung.

Josh did not wait for the verdict. Instead, he decided to offer his services in return for clemency. "I hear yore about ready to go atter Bowdry," he said. "What's yore plan?"

Rufe's fact got so red it was easy to believe he would have smoked even without the cigar, which he began chewing in a slow rage. "Don't even mention that word to me," he said.

"Hell, Rufe, you was the first one I heard talkin' about a plan," Larkin said. "When I first come over here and tried to git you to go atter Bowdry, you said we needed a plan. So I thought of one for you. You can't blame me if it didn't work."

"The hell I can't!" Rufe roared, heaving his heavy bulk up out of the chair and pointing a finger at Larkin. "You bastard, you got my brother killed!"

"All right, all right, have it yore way," Larkin said quickly. "Yore boys was doin' all right at gittin' theirselves killed 'fore I ever come over here. But I don't want to argue about it. We'll do it yore way this time. I want Bowdry dead just as much as you do. Dead or run out of the country. Ain't none of us gonna have no peace while he's around."

"We shore as hell ain't," Rufe agreed. "And it's beginnin' to look like the only way to get him is to go up there in them rocks and hunt him down. That's why we need you. You know that place better than we do."

"If you do that," Josh said, "about half of you won't come back."

"You mean about half of what's left of us!" Rufe shouted hoarsely. "If we don't get him, and purty damn quick, we're gonna all be dead! Then you can bet he'll come after you!"

"That's what I figgered," Josh said, he blue eyes clouded with dread. "If he don't already know I tried to git him killed, Lucy will tell him the next time she sees him. Wimmen can't keep nothin' to theirselves even if they know it'll cause trouble and maybe git some-body killed."

"I've knowed some men like that too," Rufe said, glaring hard at the rustler. "How did yore woman find out about it? None of us never told her, and didn't nobody else know about it except you?"

Josh shifted his feet uncomfortably, wanting to be elsewhere. "I reckon she knowed without bein' told," he said. "It's like she knows what I'm gonna do before I know about it my own self. When I left to come over here I hadn't decided to go with y'all atter Bowdry, but she already knowed that's what I'd do. She'll prob'ly go straight over there and tell him. Them pony express riders never should have been men. They should have been wimmen, the way they like to carry news and gossip."

"Why in hell didn't you hogtie her?" Rufe bellowed, his cigar jumping in his mouth.

"That ain't so easy." Josh said, rubbing the back of his neck. "That's the strongest girl I ever saw, and the best scrapper. I know she don't look it, but she is. She could whup a big fat woman without a bit of trouble."

Rufe took the cigar from his mouth and suddenly roared with laughter. "You think she could whup a big fat man?" he asked. "Send her over here. I'd love to get my hands on her."

Josh lowered his head and glared at Wadley from under his brows. "Don't talk that way, Rufe," he said in a low voice, as if hoping the big man would not hear him.

Rufe put the cigar back in his mouth and quit laughing. "I don't want yore woman," he said. "If I did, I'd go over there and take her. Not that it would be much trouble, from what I've heard. And whatever you may think, women like big fat men."

"I never said they didn't," Larkin said in a worried tone.

"Fact is," Rufe rumbled, flicking ash from his cigar, "when I heard what a purty girl yore Lucy is, I figgered she had herself a good-sized feller with some meat on his bones to keep her warm on cold nights. I felt sort of let down when I saw what a tall skinny bastard you are. But then some women ain't got no taste."

"I'm tall all right," Larkin said, resentment and malice creeping into his tone, "and I reckon I look purty skinny to a man yore size."

Rufe laughed explosively, then immediately quit laughing. He gestured with his cigar before putting it back in his mouth. "Get out of here," he said. "I'm tar'd of lookin' up at such a tall ugly bastard."

Josh turned to leave, hesitated at the door. "When we goin' atter Bowdry?" he asked.

"I'll let you know," Rufe said, sitting back down. He grinned at Larkin. "You're gonna lead the attack."

When josh got outside, he found the kid, Rex Medlin, and several others lounging near the hitchrail where his horse was.

"You tell Rufe you was gonna call me out?" Rex asked.

Josh gaped at the hard, unforgiving boy. Seemed he had enemies everywhere he turned. That did not seem right either, considering he had always tried to be friends with everyone. It seemed to him now that he had even gone out of his way to get along with his enemies. Why had they ganged up on him like this? Rufe, a man he had come to help, was already plotting to take his girl away from him when this was over.

But he wanted no trouble, especially when he was so badly outnumbered, and not near as fast on the draw as he had led folks to believe. So he managed a sickly grin and said, "Nah, I'd already forgot all about that. I figgered you had too."

Rex Medlin glanced at the others as if to say, See what I mean. No guts. Yellow clear through. He took his time rolling and lighting a Bull Durham cigarette, flipped the match at Larkin's feet and said, "Well, I shore hope you're in a fightin' mood when we go after Bowdry. I'd hate like hell to charge them rocks behind a leader who ain't got no guts."

CHAPTER 18

From his lookout in the rocks, Bowdry saw Lucy Reardon descend the west ridge on the strawberry roan, leading a sleek dark horse on a halter. She came on past the shack and halted near the waterhole, looking up at the rocks.

For once he was glad to see her, still more glad to see the horses, and he did not keep her waiting. He came out of the rocks with the Henry and glanced briefly at the dark chestnut, then met the rider's bright, direct gaze. She had bold eyes. There was no getting around it, she was a bold woman.

"I thought you might need a horse," she said. "I heard yours got shot."

"I wouldn't pay too much attention to idle talk," he said, even as he flicked another admiring glance at the chestnut gelding.

"Like him?" she asked. When Bowdry only shrugged, she added, "I'll trade him for you for this old roan."

Bowdry shook his head. "I'd better keep the roan."

"Why?" she asked. "The chestnut's a better horse."

"Better looking anyway," Bowdry said. "But I know the roan ain't stolen."

Her face reddened behind the freckles. "And you ain't sure about the chestnut, is that it?"

Bowdry merely shrugged.

"Well, as a matter of fact he is stolen," Lucy said with a little smile. "Josh stole him from Harris Thacker about a few years back. But I didn't think it would matter, you're in so much trouble already. And the Wadleys claim you stole a sorrel from them."

"That's news to me," Bowdry said. "Fact is I was sort of thinking about stealing one of their animals for shooting mine, but I hadn't got around to it yet."

"Then you shouldn't object to a stolen 3-Bar horse," Lucy said. "I'd like to keep the roan. I've sort of become attached to him. We're old friends."

"I hate to separate you," Bowdry said, studying the blunt red head of the speckled horse. "But I'd sort of like to keep him myself."

"Why?" Lucy asked, puzzlement in her eyes and voice. "You claim that old man didn't mean anything to you, so why should you care about his horse?"

"What did he mean to you?" Bowdry asked, studying her through narrow eyes.

"He was just an old man I felt sorry for," she said. "He was all alone in the world, and I know what it's like to be alone. I've been alone a lot myself."

Bowdry, who had been alone more than most, offered no comment. He looked at the chestnut. If you did not look closely, the horse looked like one of the darker shades of bay, because it had a black mane and tail. But a bay that dark would have black stockings, and this horse didn't.

"I guess it don't matter," he said after a time. "Like you say, I'm already in so much trouble, a stolen horse won't make much difference. And if I kept the roan, somebody might get the idea I killed the old man and took his horse."

Lucy threw him a startled look. Then she looked down at the roan and said, "I hadn't thought about that. Now I don't know as I want to keep him. Somebody might even think I killed the old man."

"Did you?" Bowdry asked after watching her in silence for a moment.

Her face paled behind the freckles and she studied him carefully, her eyes not as bright and bold as before. "That's not very funny," she said softly.

"What happened to that old man wasn't very funny either," Bowdry said, not quite frowning, but close to it. "Somebody around here killed him. I don't much think it was Larkin or any of the Wadley bunch, and that don't leave too many likely suspects."

"So you've eliminated the likely suspects and started in on the unlikely ones, is that it?" she asked, watching him with a still, strange look in her eyes.

Bowdry shrugged uncomfortably. "I know it sounds crazy. I only said that because I don't know of anyone else who ever even came around here. Just the Wadley bunch trying to scare him off, and you and Larkin."

"Ain't you overlooking someone?" she asked.

Bowdry looked at her curiously. "Who?"

"You," she said.

"Yes, there's me," he admitted.

"You were around here a lot just before he was killed," she said. "How do I know all this talk ain't just to draw suspicion away from yourself?"

"I imagine that's what a lot of people would think," Bowdry said.

"Did you kill him?" she asked.

Bowdry smiled faintly and shook his head. "No, I didn't kill him. Maybe a little at a time, in other ways. But I never pulled a gun on him. There were times when I wanted to. He was a cantankerous old cuss and hard as hell to get along with. But it wasn't me."

"He really was your father, wasn't he?" Lucy asked.

Bowdry's face seemed to turn to stone. "We've already been through that," he said quietly.

Lucy frowned in puzzlement. "If he wasn't your father, I don't understand why you're so determined to find the person who killed him. I realize we've been through that too, but I still don't understand it. People get killed all the time and usually nothing's ever done about it."

"That's why," Bowdry said. "It happens too much. I've about decided that anybody who can do something about it, should, especially where there's no law or the law won't do anything."

"Kill the killers, is that it?" she asked, as if a little horrified by the idea.

Bowdry nodded. "That's it."

"And what does that make you?" she asked.

"It makes me a killer," he said. "There's a difference. But if you can't see it, I can't explain it to you."

"And what happens if you're wrong?" she asked. "You thought Hunk and them other two killed Mr. Pollard, so you killed them. Then you found out it wasn't them, but they're just as dead."

Bowdry's face twisted in an expression bordering on pain, and deep lines appeared where none had been a moment before. It was the only time Lucy had seen his hard weathered face change very much. "That's why I hate to kill any more of those bastards," he said. "I'm convinced most of them need killing for other things, but I hate to do it when they think they've got right on their side."

Lucy's mouth opened in amazement. "You're a fool," she said. "They'll kill you if they get a chance and think nothing of it."

Bowdry studied her thoughtfully, the hint of a smile in his somber eyes. "What were you saying a minute ago?"

"Forget what I was saying," she told him. "Now I'm talking about staying alive. That's the only difference that makes any sense to me. This ain't the time to start worrying about your conscience or wondering if that trash needs killing. They've been trying to get you from the start. That's what Hunk and them other two were doing over here the day you killed them. Rufe sent them to kill you."

"You know that for a fact?" Bowdry asked, his voice as hard as his face.

She nodded. "Josh heard them talking about it, and he told me. So whether you knew it at the time or not, you had the best reason in the world for killing them three. If you hadn't, they would have killed you."

"Well, well," Bowdry murmured to himself. He seemed vastly relieved, as if a great load had been taken off his mind. He was almost smiling. Then he suddenly looked at Lucy and asked, "Did he hear them say anything about the old man?"

She glanced away. "Not very much. But he heard enough to know they were planning to kill Mr. Pollard if they didn't manage to scare him off. I don't think any of them knows for certain whether Hunk and them two killed him or not that night they went to town. I don't think they said anything about it, but the others ain't absolutely sure then didn't do it."

"I figured it was them, or one of them, till I realized those horse tracks had been made by Larkin's Appaloosa," Bowdry said. "It may turn out to be him after all."

"You mean Josh?"

Bowdry nodded.

Lucy pushed her long red hair back from her neck with both hands, then buttoned her denim jacket all the way to the top. The sun had set and the wind was getting colder. It was going to be a bad night.

"There's something else you should know," she said finally. "Josh went back over there. Two of them came to get him and he went with them. I think they're planning to attack this place and they want him along, I'm not sure why. I would have told you sooner, but I wanted a chance to talk to you and I was afraid you'd make me leave when you found out about that."

"It ain't just out of bad manners that I ain't asked you to get down," Bowdry said harshly, grabbing the chestnut's lead rope. "Now get out of here."

"There ain't any danger yet," she said. "Josh and them ain't much more than got over there by now. They may not bother you tonight." She studied Bowdry thoughtfully in the fading light. "Don't you ever get lonesome for a woman to talk to?"

"Women don't bother me when they ain't around," he said. "Not very much of the time anyhow."

She laughed softly, watching him with her bright gaze, everything else forgotten for the moment. "Were you ever married?" she asked.

"You sure picked a hell of a time to get on that subject," he said impatiently, watching the rocks.

"Were you?"

"I tried it once," he said.

"Didn't work out?"

"It worked out for a while," he said. "Not for very long. About half of the time I had the feeling she was blaming me for something I didn't know I'd done."

"Most women are like that," Lucy said. "I just thought everyone knew it."

"Maybe everyone else did, but I didn't." Bowdry said, scanning the bleak north ridge with somber eyes. "She went back to her people and I went back to being alone. That's the best way. For me it's the only way."

"I was sort of beginning to get that feeling," Lucy said, a little sadly. "It seems like some people were just meant to be alone. I guess you're one of them."

Bowdry's lips twisted in a wry, wistful smile. "I reckon I knew it all along. I seem to recall some such thought going through my mind when we were standing in front of that preacher. But I figured I'd better give it a try, just in case I was wrong. She was a mighty pretty girl."

"You're not bad looking yourself," Lucy said. "When I first saw you I had this silly notion of running away with you. Maybe go to some big town where there are lots of people and lots of nice things. I've only got one life and I don't want to spend it in a dead place like this."

"Afraid you picked the wrong man," Bowdry said, his eyes bleak and remote. "If I get out of here alive, I won't be going to any big town. Not to stay very long anyhow. That's about the last thing I want."

Lucy shrugged, the light in her eyes seeming to fade with the twilight. "I said it was a silly notion. I'd prob'ly feel out of place in a big town myself, I've been out here in these hills so long. But a girl can dream, can't she?"

"It ain't a silly notion," Bowdry said. "I just ain't the right man."

"I don't guess I'm the right girl either," she said after a moment. "I guess I've known for a long time that I'm not cut out for anything but the kind of life I've got now, living with a no-account rustler. Josh and I are two of a kind, I just don't like to admit it."

"You better keep him away from the Wadleys, if you want to keep him alive," Bowdry said.

"I tried to get him not to go back over there," she said. "I agreed not to come back over here anymore if he'd leave you alone and keep away from them. When he broke his promise I broke mine. I told him not to come back to the LR. But I've said that so many times he knows it don't mean anything. If he's still alive when this is over, I'll prob'ly take him back, knowing me. I guess we belong together."

"If he comes up here with that bunch trying to kill me, he may not be alive," Bowdry said in a hard tone. "I already let him go once when I should have killed him. Him and some of the others too. That won't happen again."

"I can't blame you for that," she said. "I've got a feeling I'll never see Josh alive again. And that might be the best thing that could happen, for me I mean. He's going to get us both hung with his rustling. There's already been talk of stringing us both up or running us out of the country. If I had any brains I'd get out before that happens, with or without Josh."

"I'd strongly advise that," Bowdry said in a distant tone. He had not moved yet seemed to draw farther away from her as the shadows closed around him.

Lucy looked up at the huge rocks looming in the dusk and shivered. "I'd better go. I don't want to get trapped here and have to spend the night in this place. I've been over here before at night, but it seemed different then. Now there's the smell of death in this place."

"There is death in this place," Bowdry said, "and there'll be more."

"I don't want to see it," she said. "I guess I'm not as brave as I thought I was."

"Thanks for bringing the horse," he said, getting a grip on the chestnut's halter. "I'll remember it."

"Try to stay alive," she said, as she turned the roan. "But if I find you dead the next time I come over here I'll bury you, in case that matters."

"It don't," he said. "But thanks anyway."

"Do you think you'll still be here?" she asked. "If you're still alive, I mean?"

"If I ain't, you might put a few flowers on the old man's grave now and then when you're passing by," he said. "I reckon somebody ought to."

"I'll look after his grave, if I don't decide to clear out myself." About to ride off, she hesitated, turning in the saddle to look back at Bowdry. But by then it was too dark for either to see the other clearly. "I wish you were the right man and I was the right girl," she said. "But I've got a feeling it's too late for both of us."

"I sort of had that feeling myself," Bowdry agreed.

CHAPTER 19

Bowdry watered the chestnut and led him up a dim trail to the rock-walled enclosure, then brushed out the tracks, bending close to the ground in the poor light. He did it mainly from habit, almost without thinking, for they would find the horse in any case after they killed him, those who were left. And kill him they would, if they all came at once. Nothing would save him now, no precaution, no skill, no trick or stratagem. One man, however good he might be with guns, would not stand much of a chance against a dozen.

His only hope was to saddle up and be long gone when they got here. But that he could not do, being the kind of man he was. He had never seriously considered running, and did not consider it now.

Lucy, with a woman's intuition, had known it would do no good to ask him to leave, get out while he could. She had realized that such a suggestion would amount almost to an insult.

When he had brushed out the tracks all the way back down to the waterhole, Bowdry bent down for a short drink and rose to run his glance along the dark ridge encircling the bowl. In his mind he marked the spots where he had placed the captured guns and ammunition, and mapped out the best routes to those spots from various places in the rocks, in the event he needed to rearm himself in a hurry. He rehearsed every move he would make, the way he would turn, the direction and the distance to the nearest hidden gun, how he would grab the gun and use it.

But he knew the nearest gun might be too far away, and his best insurance would be to keep plenty of loaded firearms on his person or within easy reach. With this in mind he faded back into the shadows and reappeared a short time later wearing two bandoleers of cartridges across his chest, two more pistols in his belt and the Greener shotgun strapped to his back. The Henry he carried in his hand as he prowled among the rocks that cold windy night, stopping often to watch and listen.

Once he went down toward the shack and stopped at the grave. "Old man, I sure wish you could talk," he said in a matter-of-fact tone devoid of sentiment or emotion. "I'd like to get whoever killed you before they get me. I reckon I owe you that much."

But if the old man heard he could not answer, and Bowdry went back up into the rocks on the ridge. He watched the nearby shadows and the distant darkness with eyes that were alert but unafraid, almost smiling with grim anticipation. This was the sort of thing he was good at and in spite of himself he was rather enjoying the situation. They might get him, probably would, but he would go down with his guns blazing and he would take some of them with him. Those who survived would never be quite the same afterward, would never sleep quite as well again, not because of shattered nerves. They might brag about killing him but at night his face would haunt them and they would wish to God they had never set eyes on him.

Thought of his own death did not greatly disturb Bowdry. Death still seemed far away and unreal, and he could think of it with indifference and even a strange sense of exhilaration. For a while it seemed unreal and painless, the virtual certainty of it freed him of the consequences of past mistakes and future worries. Death was the great escape, the solution to all problems.

He knew from experience however that he would feel different when the threat of violence and bloodshed became stark reality. Then cold fear would knot his guts, and life on any terms would seem like the only thing that mattered.

Barney Corvin was haunted by a face, but it was not Bowdry's face.

It was the face of the man everyone called a dude and laughed at. To Corvin there was nothing funny about Miles Hinton. He had known many deadly killers in his time, and he had no doubt that Hinton was a killer of the worst kind, one who took his victims by surprise and gave them no chance. Not because he was a coward, but simply because he preferred to avoid any unnecessary risk.

The others seemed to think Bowdry was doing all the killing and once they eliminated him their worries would be over. But Barney believed the killing would continue until not one of them was left alive.

He decided it was time to get out. So far nothing had been said about pay. He would be lucky if he received cowhand's wages for risking his neck, and he did not like the Wadleys well enough to die for them. Zeb had seemed all right when they were trapped in that old shack. But now, back with the others, he seemed just like them. And in telling about the experience, he made it seem that he, Zeb, had outsmarted the tricky and treacherous Bowdry, effected their escape and kept them alive, while Barney had just tagged along, in need of someone to look after him and make sure he did not get them both killed. Try as he might, Barney could not remember it that way.

He watched and listened while Zeb talked, and Zeb went on as if he was not even there hearing his lies. Zeb had apparently found himself a new friend—the drawling, big-toothed Josh Larkin. The others, given no chance to talk, mainly listened to these two, now and then asking a question. They were all in the rather cramped bunkhouse awaiting orders from Rufe to saddle up. As usual Rufe had the main house to himself. Even when Hunk and Gord were alive, they had slept in the bunkhouse, liking the easy companionship of "the boys" and preferring to stay as far away from their bullying older brother as possible.

From his bunk near the door Barney studied the others. The paunchy red-bearded Zeb and the toothy-grinning Josh, still standing in the aisle near Zeb's bunk, trying to outlie each other. The others were either lying on their bunks or sitting on them. The sneering hard-faced boy, Rex, who had ridden in here with Barney and his pals but now regarded them with an indifference bordering on contempt. The wild-eyed Clete, who either talked too little or too much, by turns, now listening because he had little opportunity to speak. Cob, a troubled young man, lay on his bunk blinking his red-rimmed eyes as if his mind wrestled with a problem it could not solve. On the bunk over Jenson's, lay the gray-whiskered Bones Grogan, his great tragic black eyes staring at the ceiling. The cross-eyed young man called Crom had his mouth open and his chin bent to one side as he absently picked his nose. Barney had never caught his last name. The grinning Swink brothers, Chuck and Tub, one tall and fat, the other short and chunky, with pale-bearded faces so much alike they might have passed for twins, but weren't. They were kin to the Wadleys and full-fledged members of the clan.

Someone was missing—Gil Darby. Though he had ridden with Gil for years, Barney was often unaware of his existence, and he had not noticed that Gil was not in the bunkhouse. Whether Gil talked or was silent, it was mighty easy to forget he was around, and not to notice it when he wasn't. But Barney liked the small dark man. Gil never caused any trouble, yet could be relied on when you needed him.

It occurred to Barney that no one in the bunkhouse seemed aware of *his* existence. At least no one was paying any attention to him at the moment. He quietly put on his hat and gun, left the bunkhouse in the early dusk and walked out to the corral, where he found Gil perched on the top rail like a roosting vulture, ragged and scrawny looking in the cold wind. Gil was watching the horses picking about the corral, their colors fading with the light into indistinguishable darkness. Gil liked horses better than he did people and never got tired of watching them.

"I figgered I'd find you out here," Barney said, leaning against the corral beside Gil. He was almost as tall standing on the ground as Gil was huddled on the top rail.

Gil spat tobacco juice and wiped his mouth, then hooked a thumb over his shoulder. "Gettin' a little thick in there with them two goin' at it."

Barney glanced at the bunkhouse, then at the main house, where lamplight already showed through cracks in the boarded-up office window. Rufe Wadley was still in there chewing the dead stub of his last cigar and trying to come up with a new "plan" that would work against Bowdry, though he no longer used the word or permitted anyone else to.

The boarded–up window reminded Barney that it was not safe anywhere, not even here at the ranch. He cut a sharp glance at the shadows and the dark slope beyond the corral, then said in a low tone, "I been wantin' to talk to you, Gil. I think it's time we got the hell out of here before it's too late. I ain't said nothin' to the kid. I don't think he'd want to go, and he might even give us away to get in better with this bunch here. He can't wait to go after Bowdry."

"I never trusted that kid nohow," Gil said. "It was Whitey's idea to let him tag along. He seemed to find the kid amusin'."

"That kid's about as amusin' as a mean young rattler," Barney said. "And he's gonna get what he deserves when he goes after Bowdry. But I don't think it was Bowdry follerin' me and Zeb any of the time. It was that Miles Hinton, and he meant to kill us."

Gil looked at him in surprise. "You mean that dude?"

"That ain't no dude," Barney said. "I don't know how they ever got the notion he was one. Wearin' nice clothes and washin' once in a while don't make him a dude. I bet he can ride and shoot or do anything else better'n this bunch here."

"That ain't sayin' much," Darby grunted, spitting again. "Did you ever see so many fat fellers in one place? I was surprised that Rufe could even get on a horse by hisself."

Barney again glanced at the house, then muttered, "I'd sure like to have whatever pay he figgers we got comin'. But I don't think he's got no cash money on hand, and he'd try to keep us from leavin'. Our best bet is just to sneak off without sayin' a word to nobody."

"I'm ready when you are," Gil muttered. "And I figger right now is as good a time as any. Uh-oh."

Just then the house door opened and Rufe called in his booming voice, "Who's that down there?"

"Barney and Gil," Barney said.

"Just the two I want to see!" Rufe bellowed. "Come on in here, boys! I want to talk to you!"

Barney and Gil looked at each other in alarm, wondering if Rufe meant to send them on some dangerous mission that might get them killed, just when they had been about to pull out. They crossed to the house and shuffled through the door, following Rufe into his little office room.

Rufe eased his huge bulk into the chair behind the desk. No older than Barney, and a good ten years younger than Gil, he assumed a fatherly air, stern but kind. The sternness would remain, but if crossed, the kindness would be obliterated in an explosion of rage.

He did not ask them to sit. Indeed, there was no place for them to sit. But he wore a smile meant to put them at ease. It did not. A scowl on his bloated red face would have worried them far less. For it was not like Rufe to smile at his help unless he had something pretty bad in mind for them. The "help" included everyone at the ranch, blood kin and all. "You boys ain't never been to town, have you?" he asked.

Surprised by the question, they merely shook their heads.

Rufe rubbed his plump hands together briskly. "Good! They won't know you from Adam. They'll just think you're a couple of drifters passin' through."

They just blinked in silence, wondering what he was leading up to.

"Here's what I got in mind, boys," Rufe said, getting down to business. "Bowdry has got hold of most of our guns. We ain't got no rifles, and barely enough handguns to go around. Guns are damned expensive and right now we're a little short on cash money around here. So what I want you boys to do is stick up that general store in town and bring back all the guns and ammunition you can carry, as well as any loose cash he's got on hand. Oh, and bring me a box of the best cigars he's got. I'm fresh out. You can take that kid along with you if you like. Nobody won't know him either."

Gil swallowed his tobacco juice. Barney finally found his voice and stammered, "We'd just as soon go by ourselves. Kid's sort of reckless."

Rufe smiled and nodded. "That's what I figgered. That's why I never called him in here. You boys can handle it anyway. But you better get started. That store closes around nine. If you don't make it by then you'll have to break in. We need some rifles real bad, Winchesters if he's got them, and as many handguns as you can carry. Maybe even a few shotguns."

Barney and Gil looked at each other, and then Barney said, "Well, I guess we better get started."

"You won't have no trouble findin' the way," Rufe said. "Just foller the road. It'll lead you all the way to town. But when you start back, go on north a piece and then circle wide around, in case anyone tries to foller yore trail come mornin'. I doubt if they will," he added with a grin. "Ain't no sheriff or marshal there, and them townfolks is scared of their own shader."

"Well, I guess we better get started," Barney said again. "We may be sorta late gettin' back, if we make a wide loop to throw them off our trail."

"Just try to get back before day, so nobody won't spot you," Rufe said.

They nodded and turned toward the door, anxious to get away.

"Hold on a minute," Rufe growled, losing his friendly smile. "Make it seem like you're after cash and when you don't find enough of it, pretend you just decide on the spur of the moment to take some guns. Make him think you aim to sell the guns later, so he won't get to wonderin' what you plan to do with them."

"Good idea," Barney said, while Gil chewed his tobacco in silence. "Anything else?"

"That about covers it," Rufe said, watching them with a frown. Then he suddenly smiled again. "Just don't forget my cigars. That's the most important thing."

"We won't," Barney said, following Gil outside.

Gil did not say anything until they were saddling their horses in the dark. Then he asked, "You thinkin' what I am?"

"Yep," Barney said. "But don't say nothin' till we're away from here."

Once away from the ranch buildings, following the road north along the narrow valley between the towering dark hills, they giggled like boys who had just gotten away with some clever mischief.

"What a lucky break!" Gil said in a low, excited tone. "It couldn't of worked out better if we'd planned it this way ourselves! Now they won't expect us back much 'fore mornin'. By then we'll be long gone."

"You know, I was just thinkin'," Barney said, a short time later. "That wasn't such a bad idea Rufe had. Why don't we hold up that store just like he planned, but keep the money for ourselves."

"That ain't a bad idea," Gil admitted. "We're flat broke and we need us a road stake and some grub. But what we gonna do with all them guns? They'd just slow us down."

"The hell with the guns," Barney said. "Maybe take along a couple of Winchesters in case somebody tries to foller us."

"I been wantin' me a good saddle gun," Gil said. "And I wouldn't mind havin' me one of them purty little double-action Lightnin' Colts. They fit real handy in a feller's belt, and so light you hardly even know they're there. I started to buy one once, but found I was a few dollars short. Them storekeepers tries to rob a feller ever' chance they get."

"Well, this is a good time to get even," Barney said.

In their excitement they had forgot all about Miles Hinton, the dude who liked to kill people.

Miles had returned to town for a hot meal and warmer clothes, for the wind had icy teeth in it, and would get a lot colder before the night was over. With things coming to a head out in the hills, he had decided he could not afford to spend the bad night in his room, as he would have liked to do.

As he was leaving the hotel again with the Ethan Allen shotgun in his blanket roll, he saw the two men just dismounting in front of the store across the street. He stopped just inside the hotel door to watch them. At first it was their secretive manner and the way they looked along the dark empty street that caught his attention. Then as they opened the door and entered the store he recognized them in the light. He had seen the pair that same day riding with the Wadleys.

Through the store window he saw them point guns at the storekeeper and say something. Then the short one went over toward the corner where the guns were while the tall one kept the storekeeper covered.

Hinton left the hotel and walked quietly along the deserted street, passing the store without looking toward it. But once past the store he angled over to the far side of the street and entered a dark narrow alley between two buildings. Here he stopped and, working without apparent hurry but wasting no time or motions, he took the Ethan Allen from his blanket roll, put the gun together and loaded it with buckshot. Then he stepped to the mouth of the alley and waited, his face numb in the cold wind.

Only moments later the two men left the store and started toward their horses at the rail, each carrying a rifle and a gunnysack, the short one chuckling over their loot.

Miles raised the long-barreled shotgun to his shoulder and fired the right barrel. The tall man, about to tie his sack to the saddle horn, fell against the frightened horse and slid to the ground.

In his excitement the short man dropped both rifle and grub sack and did a nervous little dance, staring at the tall man who lay on the ground almost under the feet of his plunging horse.

Hinton fired the other barrel and the short man, grabbing his middle, bent over toward him in a curiously comical bow and pitched to the ground on his face.

Hinton stepped back into the dark alley, took the shotgun apart and wrapped the two pieces back up in his blankets. When he came back out on the street he stayed in the shadows and made no noise until he was almost to the little group of excited townsmen that had gathered around the two dead men. The white-haired storekeeper stood holding the rifles and other things taken from him. He had been talking in a shaky voice but suddenly fell silent when he saw Hinton. His eyes rested for a long moment on the stiff blanket roll under Hinton's arm.

"What happened?" Hinton asked the nearest man. "I was on my way to the stable and heard shooting."

"Why, them two men held Ollie up, and then somebody killed them with a shotgun!" the man said.

"Must of been Bowdry," somebody else said. "And these two must have been riding for the Wadleys. That's how I figger it."

The townsmen fell to arguing among themselves about the identity of the killer, and Miles went on down the street toward the stable, noticed by no one except the silent storekeeper, Ollie Rice. Whether out of fear or gratitude or a curious code of his own, the storekeeper would remain silent for many years before voicing his suspicions about Miles Hinton. Perhaps he just did not think anyone would believe him, for nearly everyone was convinced that Hinton was just a harmless dude, incapable of anything either very good or very bad.

One old-timer, when told, dismissed Rice's theory as hogwash, and even suggested that old Ollie himself might have wielded the lethal shotgun on that cold windy night. Mousy little storekeepers had been known to turn into lions when somebody tried to rob them.

CHAPTER 20

By midnight Bowdry was dead tired from carrying so much weight around, trying to make sure they were not sneaking up on him from any direction. Stretching out on the hard ground for a little rest, he thought there had to be a better way.

He lay there for a while and it suddenly occurred to him that there was a better way. He sat up at once and then got to his feet, saying softly, "It just might work." He wondered why he had not thought of it sooner.

There were many natural paths through the rocks, but no more than half a dozen that an attacking party would be likely to choose. At some point all these paths led between boulders or rock outcroppings where there was barely room for one man to pass. In the dark that man would not notice a string across the path, especially if it was hidden by a bush, whether it grew there naturally or had been transferred there for the purpose.

Bowdry had some twine in his saddlebags and there was more down at the shack. He rigged a cocked gun along each of the five most likely paths, with a string tied to the trigger and running across the trail a little above the ground. In every case, the string was concealed by brush or weeds and so was the gun.

In four of the places he had a pistol with a single cartridge in the chamber under the hammer. But on the most likely path he rigged the Greener so that both barrels would go off if the string was tripped, and the man who tripped the string would never know what hit him.

His load considerably lightened—also the load on his mind—Bowdry lay down in the rocks to get some much-needed sleep.

Over at the 3-Bar bunkhouse nine other men slept like bears, having been told the attack was off for tonight. But up at the main house a kerosene lamp smoked and a fat man paced, the unlighted stub of a cigar clamped between his teeth. As he paced the fat man muttered to himself. "Ain't light yet, but they should be back. Reckon I should of told the fools to circle around the Pollard place, but I figgered they'd know that much by now." The fat man's voice suddenly rose to an enraged bellow, and those down at the bunkhouse were shaken out of a sound sleep. "I got to do the thinkin' for ever'body! Ain't nobody else around here got brains enough to ride facin' the front!"

The fat man stepped to the door, opened it and roared, "Zeb!"

"What!" Zeb howled back in a tone of outrage, not liking to have his sleep shattered that way.

"Get up here, that's what!" Rufe boomed and slammed the door, partly in anger and partly because he had become concerned about night prowlers with shotguns. A load of buckshot in the gut was something he did not need right now on top of everything else.

Down at the bunkhouse Zeb cried as he tugged on his boots, "What in hell does he want at this time o' night?"

"Tell him to hold it down up there," Josh said, pulling the blankets back up over his face. "Unless I git a few hours' sleep, I ain't no good the next day."

"Better watch out when you go out there, Zeb," old Bones Grogan muttered. "Bowdry may be layin' for you with that shotgun."

"He better not be," Zeb said. "If I git shot 'cause that fat rascal gits a wild hair this time o' night—"

"Them two ain't got back with them guns yet?" Clete asked, sitting up on his bunk and looking around in the dark.

"I don't see them," Zeb said. "That's prob'ly what it's about. They should be back by now, 'less somethin' went wrong."

"If he wants you to go see about them, I'll go with you," Josh said.

"That may not even be it," Zeb said, reaching for his gunbelt, then remembering he no longer had one. "Anybody want to loan me a gun?" he asked.

"You can take mine," Cob said.

"We needed them guns," Clete said.

Zeb buckled on the borrowed gunbelt, drew the gun from the holster and checked it by feel. He stood near the door, dreading to go out. "Well, I better go up there and find out what he wants."

"So long, Zeb, if we don't never see you again," Chuck said, giggling.

Old Bones Grogan cleared his throat. "It ain't no laughin' matter. Any of us could be next. He killed Pink Deeble right here in this bunkhouse, didn't he? And Pink never hurt nobody."

"Not unless they were littler than him," Tub said. "He used to beat me up when he was nine and I was five."

"Zeb!" Rufe roared.

"You better get on up there, Zeb," Chuck said. "You keep old Rufe waitin' much longer, you'll have to go runnin' to Bowdry for protection."

Zeb opened the door carefully, stepped outside and ran for the main house.

"You took yore time," Rufe growled.

"What you want?" Zeb asked, still drowsy and irritable.

"Hell, them two ain't got back yet and it'll soon be daylight." Rufe said. "Somethin' must of gone wrong. Saddle up and go see if you can find them, or find out what happened to them."

"Why me?" Zeb asked, frowning.

"I heard you down there braggin' how you outsmarted Bowdry and give him the slip," Rufe said. "Maybe you can do it again, checkin' that stretch of road along there for bodies."

"I ain't goin' by myself," Zeb said.

"Then take somebody with you."

"Josh said he'd go."

"Not him," Rufe said. "He might not come back."

"The Swink boys just volunteered," Zeb said.

Zeb halted his horse before they got to what he considered the most dangerous stretch of road. It was still dark, with only a hint of gray in the east, and bitter cold, too cold for the time of year. But the wind had died down and in the frosty stillness every rock and stunted tree crouched as if ready to leap at them.

"Which one of us is the biggest and toughest and the best fighter?" Zeb asked.

"I reckon I am," Chuck said. "Why?"

"Good," Zeb said. "You go first."

"What's wrong, Zeb?" Tub asked. "You scared?"

"I don't mind goin' first," Chuck said cheerfully. "You boys stay behind me and if I get it in the gut, you hightail it back to the ranch and tell Rufe to come hisself the next time."

The big man took the lead, riding boldly ahead, and Zeb and Tub fell behind him, riding abreast.

Tub rode in frowning silence for a few moments. The short, stout young man had a ready sense of humor but he also had a bad temper at times, and he felt strangely protective toward his big brother, who was strong as an ox and let people take advantage of him because of it, always giving him the hardest job.

"I don't like it," Tub said. "Back there at the bunkhouse you let on like you was just itchin' for another chance at Bowdry. Now you want Chuck to ride up front where he'll get it first if we run into a ambush."

"I said I don't mind," Chuck said, though he sounded less cheerful than before. "Rufe put Zeb in charge. It's only right we should do like he says."

"I still don't like it," Tub said.

"Nobody's stoppin' you from ridin' up there with him," Zeb said flatly.

"You stay back there, Tub," Chuck said. "No use both of us gettin' it, and I don't want you to get hurt if I can help it."

"I don't want you to get hurt neither," Tub said. "If Zeb's in charge, he should be the one ridin' up front. I thought that was where leaders usually were—in the lead."

"Well, it's a little different around here, I reckon," Chuck said, sounding less and less happy about the whole thing, as he watched the dark rocks and trees on either side of the road. "I reckon you've noticed Rufe don't hardly ever take no chances hisself. He just sends somebody else. When he goes, he takes the whole bunch along to protect him."

"That don't give Zeb no right to put you up there," Tub insisted.

"I've heard about enough out of you," Zeb said in a hard, angry tone. "Chuck thought it was mighty funny when he thought Rufe meant to send me by myself. That's why I put him up front."

"You know I was only jokin', Zeb," Chuck said unhappily.

"Right," Zeb snapped. "You was only jokin'. You thought it was funny. How funny is it now, Chuck?"

Miles Hinton had spent a miserable night shivering in some brush near the road, with the double-barreled Ethan Allen standing against a rock in easy reach. He had slept very little, but toward morning he dozed off, to be awakened in the false dawn by the muffled sound of horses coming along the road.

Rising and reaching for the shotgun, he saw that there were three riders and they were no more than thirty yards away. The big man in the lead he took to be Rufe Wadley, and his heart raced with excitement. This, he told himself as he raised the shotgun to his shoulder, was his lucky day.

When he drew the right hammer back he already had the gun aimed at the man's broad middle, and he did not give them time to react to the warning click, clearly audible in the breathless hush. He squeezed the trigger, the gun leapt and roared, and the big man slumped in the saddle.

One of the riders behind wheeled his horse and galloped back down the road.

The other, a short chunky man, cried out, "Chuck!" and reined his animal toward the wounded man.

Chuck was bent over in the saddle holding his middle. "Get outta here!" he yelled hoarsely. "Go on, dammit! I'm done for anyway!"

"Not a chance!" the short one said, grabbing the reins of Chuck's horse. "Hang on, Chuck! I'll get you outta here!"

But as he turned the horses, the big one slipped from the saddle and fell heavily to the ground. The short one jerked the horses to a halt and swung down, going toward Chuck and trying to help him to his feet.

"No, Tub!" Chuck said. "Don't mind me! Get outta here 'fore he kills you too! He's just there in that brush!"

But the short man bent under the big one and stumbled toward the horses with him.

The horses, frightened by the shot and the smell of blood, raised their heads in the air and rolled their eyes at the strange creature lurching toward them. Suddenly the two animals wheeled and thundered back down the road after the other horse and rider.

"Zeb!" the short man yelled. "Stop the horses!"

"Ain't no use!" Chuck said in a weakening voice. "He won't bring them horses back. Duck in them cedars and don't stop runnin', Tub. It's yore only chance. Hurry, now!"

But Tub was still staring back down the road and he yelled again, "Zeb!"

Hinton, surprised that the big man was not Rufe Wadley, was now crouched in the brush, watching the pair in amazement, but without any feeling of sympathy. They were the kind who made fun of him behind his back. The short one stood there in the road swaying under the weight of the big one, when he should have dropped him and dived for the rocks.

When Hinton cocked the left hammer, the short one did start for the rocks, but he was still carrying the big one and moving too slow. Much too slow.

Zeb was moving very fast. He galloped into the 3-Bar yard yelling hoarsely, "Git yore guns! Bowdry's atter me!"

He leapt from the skidding horse and ran for the door of the main house, thinking Rufe could protect him if anyone could.

Rufe was suddenly there in the door before him with a huge pistol, blocking his way. Staring past Zeb, Rufe saw two riderless horses gallop into view. They made straight for the corral and tried to get in at the closed gate. Rufe watched and listened for some moments, but heard no other horse coming.

Red-faced with anger, he glared at Zeb. "Bowdry, hell," he said. "Wasn't nothin' atter you but the Swink boys' horses."

Zeb's face was also red, but with embarrassment. He was aware of men pouring out of the bunkhouse with their guns in their hands as he said, "It was too dark back there to tell and I just thought it was Bowdry chasin' me."

"What happened?" Rufe barked.

Zeb was breathing hard and his voice shook. "Bowdry ambushed us with that shotgun. Chuck got it the first thing and I reckon Bowdry got Tub too when he tried to help Chuck git away."

"You mean you don't even know whether Tub got shot or not?" Rufe asked.

"Not for shore," Zeb said. "It was still too dark to see anything much. But I heard that shotgun go off twice, and I never heard Tub shoot back, so him and Chuck both are prob'ly dead."

"How the hell is it you're always the one who gets away?" Rufe asked.

"I don't know," Zeb said uncomfortably, not looking at Rufe or any of the others who were gathering around to listen, blank-faced with shock. "I was just lucky, I guess."

"Lucky, hell," Rufe said. "You can't blame it on luck. Not when it keeps happenin' like this. First you run off and let Gord get killed, now them two." Then he asked, "What about Barney and Gil? You see anythin' of them?"

Zeb shook his head. "But I figger Bowdry ambushed them farther along the road there. He must hang out around there a lot, waitin' for us to ride by."

"He shore must," Rufe agreed, his face congested with a growing rage. "That son of a bitch tells us not to come near his place. Keep on the road, he says. Then he hangs out near the road and fills us full of buckshot when we go by!"

Rufe had started out quiet, but by the time he finished his voice roared and shook like thunder. He pounded one fat hand with the other fist. "Saddle up, you sons of bitches! We're goin' after him while there's still some of us left!"

Josh Larkin's mouth fell open in surprise. "You mean in broad daylight?"

Rufe gave the big-toothed man a look of withering scorn. "That's exactly what I mean. I know how we can get in them rocks without gettin' shot all to hell, and once we're in the rocks he don't stand a chance against all of us. At night he might get away, but not in the daytime, 'cause I aim to stay down below and make shore he don't get away. You"—he pointed at Larkin—"will lead the attack up in the rocks. You and Zeb."

CHAPTER 21

Avoiding the road, they circled through the cedar hills and halted behind the crest of the hill just east of Bowdry's rocky ridge.

"All right, Larkin," Rufe boomed, lighting the cigar stub he had been saving. "Take yore three men and circle around. We'll wait here and get Bowdry's attention so you'll have a chance to get in them rocks on the west side. You'll be leadin' the attack from that side. If you try to chicken out, my men have got orders to shoot you theirselves."

Josh's usually ruddy face was pale and his big teeth were bared in a kind of grimace, as if he hated himself for getting into a predicament like this. But his drawling voice was calm enough. "I won't chicken out. I want Bowdry dead just as much as you do."

Rufe nodded shortly, and Larkin led out around the side of the hill followed by Cob Jenson, Bones Grogan and the cross-eyed Crom. All four were silent and looked like men going to their doom.

Rufe, huge in a dark overcoat, sat his horse on the shoulder of the hill and smoked his short cigar stub, now and then taking it from his mouth to flick the ash and see how much of the cigar was left. Once or twice he glanced narrowly at the other three men but for the most part ignored them. There was not much wind today, but the sun shone through a dull haze and the hills seemed dark with shadows.

Rufe suddenly looked at Zeb's red-bearded face and said in a mocking tone, "Bowdry's atter me."

The mean-faced boy, Rex, sneered at Zeb, but said nothing.

Clete was checking his gun, a wild glitter in his eyes that might have been either fear or ferocity.

Zeb's drawn face got a little redder, but did not change otherwise and his eyes, pinched together in somber reflection, did not shift toward his fat cousin. He was used to Rufe's jibes. "You can make fun all you like," he said. "But I ain't seen you goin' atter Bowdry. You keep sendin' the rest of us to git our heads shot off."

Surprisingly, Rufe showed no anger. Instead, he let out a booming laugh. "What the hell you think I keep you boys around for?" he asked.

"I'm beginin' to wonder," Zeb said. "I don't think you care much if all the rest of us do git killed. Then you'll have that ranch all to yoreself."

"I already got it all to myself," Rufe said. "Harris Thacker signed it over to me, just me. Yore name ain't included, Zeb, and bein' a cousin shore as hell don't make you no partner."

Zeb's face heated with anger behind the short red beard. "Then why in hell don't you pay us once in a while, if we ain't yore partners? All this time you been lettin' us think we had a share in the ranch and the stock, just to git us to work for nothin'."

"A place to stay, two or three meals a day, and good horses to ride—you call that nothin'?"

"Ain't nobody else works that cheap," Zeb said. "If we ain't got no share in the ranch, then by God you're gonna start payin' us for our work, and I don't mean just a few dollars once or twice a month when we go to town."

Rufe moved his heavy shoulders in a shrug. "Ain't nobody forcin' you to stay, Zeb. You can leave anytime."

"Good," Zeb said, gathering the reins in his fat red hands. "This is as good a time as any."

"*After* we get Bowdry," Rufe said. "You try runnin' out on me now and I'll shoot you down like a yeller dog."

Zeb's lips twitched in bitter frustration and for a moment he looked as if he might cry. He was better with a gun than Rufe would ever be, and there were times when he would have enjoyed putting a bullet in his fat, bullying cousin, who so loved to throw his weight around and trample on those around him. This was one of those times. But Zeb knew he wouldn't do it and Rufe knew he wouldn't, and was enjoying the spectacle of Zeb's silent struggle with himself, knowing beforehand what the outcome would be. Zeb might talk but he would not do anything. He did not have Rufe's guts or his ruthlessness.

Rufe's cigar had gone out. He flicked away the ash and put the stub back in his pocket. "Them others have had time to circle around," he said. "When we get up to the top of this hill here and get Bowdry's attention, I want you three to start straight toward that ridge, but cut to the right when you're just out of rifle range and circle around till you're about where the ridge curves or a little farther, then spread out and ride like hell for them rocks. That'll give them others a chance to get in the rocks on the west side."

"I figgered you'd give us the hard part," Zeb said.

Rufe smiled maliciously at him. "That's 'cause I figger you boys are better, or at least I figger Clete and Rex are. And you, Zeb, you seem to be mighty good at gettin' out of tight spots. Others get pushed over cliffs or get their tails shot off, but you come back without a scratch. Well, maybe you'll get back this time without a scratch. But I don't want you to come back sayin' Bowdry's atter you again. And I don't want to hear he's been chasin' you around up there in them rocks. I want to hear you been chasin' him, and this time you better bring back some live witnesses to back up yore story."

Rufe nodded curtly, giving Zeb no chance to answer. "Let's get started."

He led the way to the top of the hill and halted again. His voice roared through the hills like a sudden clap of thunder on a still day.

"Hey, Bowdry!"

Bowdry could see horses and riders in the trees and rocks on the hilltop, but he could not tell how many there were. He had a feeling, however, that this was it, the big attack he had been expecting.

"You wanted a fight, Bowdry!" Rufe bellowed, his voice seeming to obliterate the distance between them and to reverberate in the rocks around Bowdry. "Well, you got one!"

Three riders came pounding down the hill, the hoofs of their horses kicking up dust in the cedars, and Rufe still sat his bright red horse at the top, waving his arm and urging them on with his bull voice, tongue-lashing Zeb for falling behind the others. That made four. Where were the others?

Bowdry jacked a shell into the Henry and scanned the slope for the ones who should have been there but weren't, while keeping track of the three riders out of the edges of his vision. When they were almost in range he raised the rifle to his shoulder, his face grim and hard, and no mercy left in his heart. But at a roared command from Rufe they suddenly turned their horses and raced around the side of the hill, angling toward the rocky ridge but still keeping out of range.

Cussing softly, Bowdry ran along the ridge, stopped and fired at the nearest rider. But there was not time to aim and the man made it into the rocks unhit. The old Henry jammed and a moment later the other two also reached the cover of the boulders, dived off their horses and scrambled up the ridge on foot. Bowdry knew he had his work cut out for him now.

A few minutes earlier, Josh and the three men with him leapt from their galloping horses at the foot of the west ridge and Larkin led the way up the steep, boulder-strewn slope, both white-handled guns cocked and ready, his face tense with dread. His lips were pulled back from his teeth and he kept wincing in expectation of a bullet.

Suddenly he sat down on a rock, breathing heavily. "Got to git somethin' outta my boot. Y'all go on ahead. I'll catch up in a minute.

Crom shook his head. "Rufe said fur you to lead us and fur us to shoot you iff'n you tried to chicken out."

"It's all right," Larkin assured him. "Rufe won't never know the difference, and I just got to git this thorn outta my boot."

"We'll wait," old Bones Grogan said.

"It don't matter," Cob said. "This ain't his fight, not by rights. Rufe never had to take his advice."

"He shore as hell never," Larkin agreed, looking up in surprise and gratitude. He watched the three tramp by him, Jenson now in the lead. They moved along the narrowing path between two outcroppings of rock.

Just then they heard the crash of the Henry from the east ridge, and Larkin said, "Bowdry's way over there. You boys ain't got a thang to worry about."

A moment later there was a deafening blast and Cob fell back against Crom, who turned and clawed his way past a badly shaken, wild-eyed Bones. But the old man, although expecting another shattering blast, grabbed Jenson and dragged him back along the narrow curving path between the two rock outcroppings to where Larkin was frantically tugging his boot back on in preparation for flight himself. If it was to be retreat, Josh had no intention of bringing up the rear and maybe getting it from behind.

Then reason took hold of him. "Wait a minute," he said. "Bowdry can't be in two different places at the same time."

"Maybe that was one o' them boys shootin' as they charged the ridge," Bones said.

"Naw, that was that Henry," Larkin said.

"Maybe they's two of him," Crom said.

Bones had eased Cob to the ground and was looking down in horror at the young man. "He's dead," old Bones said in disbelief. "Cob is dead."

"That would have been you, Josh, iff'n you was in the lead like Rufe said," Crom told him. "I don't like you fur that, Josh. Cob, he was the only one I liked, and now he's dead because of you."

Larkin ignored the cross-eyed young man. "I got me a hunch I know what happened," he said. "That was a shotgun. I bet Bowdry had it rigged so it'd go off when somebody walked into a string or somethin'. I've heard about people gittin' shot that way when they break in houses."

"I bet he's got guns fixed to go off all over this ridge," Bones said in a hoarse, cracked voice. "We won't be able to take a step without maybe causin' another one to go off."

"You better go in front like Rufe said, Josh, unless you want me to tell him," Crom said.

"I ain't worried about him right now," Larkin said. "I never should of even come over here. Now I aim to head right back down that ridge like we come so I won't set off no more guns."

Crom raised his long-barreled pistol, cocked it with his other hand, and pointed it at Larkin. "No, you ain't neither, Josh," he said. "You done got Cob killed. Now you gonna go ahead of us on up this ridge here like Rufe said, or I'll shoot you myself. That's what he said to do."

Larkin gaped at the cross-eyed fool. "You mean you'd actual shoot me?"

"Yes, I would too, Josh," Crom said slowly, groping for the right words. He was not very bright, but he had one thought lodged in his brain—to do, as always, what Rufe said. For he feared Rufe more than he feared anything else on earth, including Bowdry and guns just waiting to go off if you tripped on a string. "It's what Rufe said to do."

Josh sat on the rock with a baffled, bewildered look on his face. He could not understand it. Seemed like just about everyone wanted to kill him, and not too long ago he had thought everyone liked him, except for Harris Thacker and a few cold-faced ranchers north of town. And, of course, old man Pollard. Maybe a few others, but certainly not everyone he met, like now.

"It's yore own fault, Josh, for gittin' Cob killed," Crom told him.

"If it hadn't been him it would have been me!"

"That's different. You was supposed to be up front, like Rufe said."

"Rufe ain't my boss!"

"He is now, while you're with us," Crom said. "He's ever'body's boss."

"This ain't gettin' us nowhere," Bones said. "Put away that gun, you fool," he told Crom, "or be ready to use it where it counts."

But Crom stubbornly shook his head. "I won't neither put it away. You ain't my boss, Bones. Rufe is, and he said for us to shoot Josh if he didn't go up front and lead us."

"He never meant it, you fool!" old Bones said, turning angrily on the half-wit. "He was only tryin' to scare Josh! You ain't even got brains enough to be up here! Now give me that gun before you get somebody killed."

What the old man did next suggested that he might not have been too bright himself. He grabbed for the gun in Crom's hand and the gun went off. The old man grunted in surprise and staggered back. He fell and lay on his back holding his middle and gasping for breath. He raised his gray-whiskered face and stared at Crom with bitter accusing eyes, then fell back dead.

"You killed him, you fool!" Josh cried.

Crom again cocked the gun, awkwardly using his left hand. 'You just set there, Josh. Don't you try nothin'."

"You killed him!" Larkin said again in disbelief.

"It was his own fault. He never should of tried to grab my gun like that. I never meant fur it to go off. But I'll shoot you if I have to. That's what Rufe said fur me to do."

"You're crazy!"

"You can say that if you want to. But you and me are goin' on to look fur Bowdry, and you're gonna go up ahead of me like Rufe said."

"You're gonna git us all killed!" Josh cried hoarsely. "I can't worry about you and Bowdry and guns set to go off, all at the same time."

"That ain't my fault." Crom pointed the long-barreled pistol at him, holding it in both hands. "You go on ahead of me now, Josh, like Rufe said."

Bowdry heard the shotgun go off, then, moments later, the pistol. That explained where the others were, trying to sneak up on his blind side, and he hoped they wiped themselves out on his unmanned guns. That seemed unlikely, however, for they would start being more careful and watch for the hidden strings which, when tripped, triggered the guns. And he had only put two guns on the west side, one a pistol that would likely miss its intended target. But he was reasonably confident that the shotgun had accounted for at least one of the attacking party.

The three on this side, still separated, were slipping through the rocks toward him. He had caught occasional glimpses of them, but had held his fire, waiting for a better shot and not wanting to give his position away.

He decided to dispense with the Henry, for he was afraid it would jam again, or misfire at a bad moment. The old gun had not been cared for and was about worn out. But Bowdry did not really need it for close fighting in the rocks, where his pistols would be easier to handle and more effective. So he hid the Henry in some brush and drew his Russian, the most accurate handgun then made.

At that moment he heard the roar of a gun off to his right and below him on the north ridge. Somebody had tripped another string, discharging one of the hidden guns.

It was Zeb. Moving carefully along one of the natural paths through the rocks with his gun cocked and ready, but not really expecting trouble yet, he kicked the string without seeing it and the gun roared from some dead looking brush near the trail, about ten feet above him. He felt the scorching breath of the bullet on his right cheek and he threw himself violently to one side, slamming into a boulder he had not noticed was so close. He bounced off the rock with a hurt shoulder and tumbled back down the steep slope as if he had been shot. Bowdry and the others, hearing him, assumed he had been.

Clete and Rex, surprised at the location of the shot, turned and began working their way silently through the rocks in that direction, moving farther away from the man they were looking for.

It was Clete who discovered the string across the path and followed it to the hidden gun. He got the gun and loaded it with shells, then called softly, "Hey, Zeb. You hit bad?"

"That you, Clete?" Zeb asked, coming back up the path, his face flushed with anger. "What in hell you shootin' at me for?"

"It wasn't me," Clete said, and showed him the string and the gun. "It wasn't nobody. Just a gun."

"I'll be damned," Zeb said. "Scared me half to death."

The kid, Rex, suddenly appeared, startling them.

"You tryin' to git yore fool head blowed off?" Zeb asked, lowering his gun.

The boy grinned unpleasantly. "No, but if I was Bowdry, both of you would be dead."

"I reckon now we know what that shootin' over yonder was about," Zeb said. "Them others run into some more guns Bowdry had put out. He's prob'ly got all them guns he tuck from us scattered through these rocks, just waitin' to go off when we run into a string. How in hell we gonna find him without gettin' shot? That bullet come so close I heard it go by."

"It's simple," Rex said, still grinning. He seemed to be enjoying this as if it were a game. "We crawl. Then if one of them guns goes off, the bullet will go above us. I don't reckon he's got them aimed at the ground."

"I hadn't thought of that," Zeb said. "But I shore do hate to crawl."

"It beats dyin'," Clete said, already getting down on his hands and knees. "This is the safest way anyhow."

"The slowest way," the kid said. "We'll have to spread out again, or we won't never find him."

"Be careful who you shoot at," Zeb said. "Or we'll be shootin' at each other."

"Anybody shoots at me will get shot at," the boy said, moving away through the rocks.

The other two noticed that he was not crawling, but walking, and they wondered about it, but said nothing.

Rex was not crawling because he was in a hurry. He wanted to find Bowdry before anyone else did.

He wanted to be the one who killed Bowdry.

CHAPTER 22

A slow, careful step at a time, Josh made his way through the jumble of rocks above the head of the canyon. This sort of thing was not for him, and he longed to turn around and go back the way he had come, find his horse and get the hell out of here. But every time he sneaked a look over his shoulder, that stubborn young fool Crom was right behind him with that big pistol pointed at his back.

Josh had his own guns in his hands, cocked and ready for use. He had about decided to use them on Crom the first chance he got. If it was not for Crom, he could still sneak out of here and go home. Let the others worry about Bowdry, and Rufe could paw the ground and bellow about it all he wanted to. This, as Josh saw it, was not his fight.

It had been bad enough to begin with when he had three men with him. Now two of them were dead and he would be better off without the other. In a fight with Bowdry, Crom would just get in the way. And very likely, trying to fire past Josh, Crom would shoot him in the back without meaning to, if he did not do it on purpose.

It was more and more clear to Josh that he had to rid himself of the cross-eyed young man following him. If he could just catch Crom off guard for a moment...

Carefully turning his head, he looked around at Crom, and his heart started pounding. For Crom did not seem to be watching him, but to be looking off down the canyon someplace, his heavy-lidded narrow eyes and swarthy round face giving him a faintly Oriental look. Josh decided this might be the best chance he would have, for time was running out. He tensed and got a good grip on his guns, preparing to whirl and fire.

Then he suddenly realized that he had been looking at the wrong eye. Crom's left eye did appear to be looking down toward the canyon. But the right eye was watching Josh closely, suspiciously. Josh let his breath out and went limp, feeling clammy and sick at the realization of how close he had come. There was no way he could have turned around and got his shot off in time, when all Crom had to do was pull the trigger.

"Don't you try nothin', Josh," Crom said. "If you turn around with them guns, I'll have to shoot you."

"What's gonna happen if you trip on a rock and fall?" Larkin asked hoarsely. "You're liable to shoot me without meanin' to."

"I won't neither," Crom said. "I'll be real careful. You just watch for them strings that make the guns go off."

"How the hell can I, with you follerin' me around and pointin' that damn cannon at my back?"

"This here's a good gun," Crom said. "It shoots nearly ever' time. One time I killed a rabbit with it. Even Rufe said that was good shootin'."

"I bet he et the rabbit too, didn't he?"

"Not all of it. He let me have some of it. But there wasn't none left for the others."

Josh suddenly stopped, with one foot half lifted to take a step. He eased the foot back down where it was and stood looking down at a small gray bush that seemed out of place somehow.

"What's wrong?" Crom asked. "You find somethin'? One time I found a old knife that way. I was just walkin' along and saw it lyin' on the ground, all rusty. Later on I lost it again."

Larkin eased the hammer down on one gun and holstered it, and slowly squatted on his heels, studying the bush.

"You find one o' them strings?" Crom asked.

"I ain't shore yet," Larkin said.

"It's a good thing you was in front," Crom said. "I never would of noticed nothin'."

Larkin saw the string under the bush, but he did not move or say anything at once. He was almost afraid to move, afraid that if he touched anything the hidden gun would go off. He did not know where the gun was or where it was pointed. But he figured that if he and Crom lay flat on the ground...

Then a sudden thought occurred to him. Maybe this was the chance he had been hoping for. If the bullet hit Crom, it would be a very lucky break for Josh.

"Stay where you are and don't move till I tell you, Crom. I want to take a closer look at this thang."

Josh himself eased back a little and lay face down on the ground, facing the bush. He reached his hand forward slowly, took hold of the bush and—

The sudden roar was loud and startling, even to Larkin who had expected it. The explosion nearly busted his ear-drums and started a terrible ringing in his ears. But Crom was even more unfortunate. The bullet caught him squarely in the chest and knocked him staggering back. He lost his gun in the fall and flapped around like a chicken with its head cut off.

Josh scrambled to his feet and ran past the poor man, almost stepping on him and laughing in wild exultation. By God, now he was free! He could get the hell out of here and go back to the LR, show Lucy she was not rid of him yet, not by a long shot. He had a feeling she would be disappointed to see him, but that would make his homecoming all the sweeter. Already he felt as if he had been away for weeks.

He suddenly stopped, his face heating with anger. Lucy might not even be at the ranch, for all he knew. And even if she was, she would be running back over here to see Bowdry the first chance she got. They would be talking about him behind his back and she would tell Bowdry what a sorry son of a bitch Josh was.

"By God, that's got to stop!" he said aloud. "No, I ain't goin' back to the ranch! Not till Bowdry's dead! If they don't git him, I aim to!"

He walked back by Crom, so absorbed in his violent thoughts

that he did not even notice the dying man. Talking to himself, Larkin went on along the crooked path through the rocks to look for Bowdry.

Bowdry heard the report of the gun and hoped the bullet had hit its target. He needed all the help he could get. He thought it possible that those hidden guns with the strings tied to the triggers might mean the difference whether he got out of this alive or not. Even if they did not kill or wound anyone, they were helping him to keep track of the movements of the Wadley men. But now there could not be more than two of the guns still unfired and there might be only one. Once fired, the guns would be harmless to the enemy and could even be used by them if they had the right kind of ammunition. They might even stumble onto some of the other guns Bowdry had hidden, the ones not set to go off, but loaded and ready for instant use, with a belt of cartridges handy.

Bowdry would not have minded having the Greener with him, but it was way over on the west ridge, out of reach. But at least it was now empty and useless to the Wadley men, for it was unlikely that they had brought along any shells for it.

Bowdry had picked the best spot he could find and was waiting for them to come to him. He knew that if he moved he might be seen or heard, and he wanted to see them first, or at least one of them. After he got the first one, he would have to move.

He was protected on three sides by boulders or rock outcroppings, with gaps between through which he could see and shoot. Behind him, offering some concealment was a low twisted cedar that stirred now and then in the breeze. Bowdry could hear the rustle of the cedar and feel the cool breath of the wind on the back of his neck, but at other times he was conscious of the growing warmth of the sun. He had taken off his long black coat because he did not need it and it hampered his movements somewhat. He kept on his light corduroy coat because, while it would not stop bullets, it somehow made him feel more secure, less exposed.

The long black coat he had placed over a rock, partly screened by brush, a little distance away. He doubted if it would fool anyone, but it was worth a try.

Even as he was thinking about the black coat, he heard a little whisper of sound off to his left and then the sudden roar of a gun. He heard the bullet hit the rock, the sound muffled by the coat, and he knew his ruse had worked.

Giving the shooter no time to discover his mistake, or recover from his surprise, Bowdry rose with his gun ready and fired the instant he saw the hard-faced boy. The boy was peering through the brush at the black coat, and blinking in wonder, and he had no time to bring his gun around and fire at Bowdry. He started the move, as quick as a striking rattler, but Bowdry's bullet spun him around in the other direction. He fell against a rock and slid down it to the ground, dropping his gun.

The boy fumbled for his gun and Bowdry, walking forward, shot him again. The boy grunted at the shock of the bullet and the gun slipped from his fingers. When Bowdry stood over him the boy raised a face that was tense and contorted in a terrible struggle. But he grinned up at Bowdry and whispered, "You ain't got a prayer. They'll kill you, and I hope they do."

Bowdry did not say anything. He silently watched the boy die, and he did not feel anything except a grim resolve to get as many more of them as he could before they killed him. And when it came to that, he had his doubts whether there were enough of them left to get the job done.

"Hell's goin' on up there?" Rufe bellowed, thinking nothing of the fact that he was nearly a half mile away. He was used to shouting orders from a great distance, and getting results. But now no one answered him. "Y'all ain't got Bowdry yet?"

Still no answer. So apparently Bowdry was still alive, and Rufe's men were keeping quiet so as not to give themselves away.

Rufe took out his stub of cigar and fired it up. Just then he heard a horse walking toward him through the rocks and cedars off to his right, and he glared that way, expecting to see one of his men slinking back with a scratch or just scared half to death. But it was only that fancy dude, Miles Hinton.

"What the hell you doin' back out here?" Rufe asked, half annoyed and half amused. "I thought I told you to stay out of these hills, 'fore you get yore fool head shot off.'"

The dude reined in abreast him, off a little to his right. "I heard shooting," he said. "Is there a fight going on up there in those rocks?"

"There shore is, son," Rufe said, smiling indulgently. It seemed only natural for him to call Hinton "son," although the latter was no younger than himself and might even have been a few years older. But he seemed so young and green, and Rufe had been head of the Wadley clan for so long that he felt like a middle-aged man. "There's one hell of a fight goin' on up there in them rocks," he added.

Hinton's glassy gray eyes gleamed with interest as he gazed at the steep rocky ridge. "That's what I figured," he said. "Do you think they'd mind if I rode up there where I can see better?"

"Why, no," Rufe assured him, his smile getting even broader. He was puffing at his cigar stub to get it going better. "You just ride right on up in them rocks to the top o' that ridge and watch the fight long as you got a mind to. They won't mind a bit."

"Good," Hinton said. "I believe I will then, if it's all right with you."

"I don't mind neither, son," Rufe said, with a generous wave of his cigar. "You go right ahead on. But don't you go blamin' me now if you get yore head shot off."

"I don't think there's much danger of that," Hinton said, lifting the reins. "Oh, by the way, Harris Thacker asked me to give you a message. He said you shouldn't have taken his cigars. He said it was bad enough when you forced him to sign the ranch over to you without paying him a penny for it. But when you made him leave his cigars behind and he knew you'd be smoking them in his house, at his office desk where he spent so much time—he said that was when he made up his mind that you weren't going to get away with it."

Rufe's broad grin was replaced by a dark scowl. He took the shredded inch of cigar from his mouth and looked at it. "I don't understand. Where did you see Harris Thacker?" Rufe's scowl got even blacker. "You mean he come by the hotel, runnin' his blab about our little deal? Sayin' I cheated him or somethin'?"

"I wasn't here then," Miles said. "I saw Harris Thacker in another hotel in Carson City. But I wasn't working there as no desk clerk." Hinton watched Rufe for a moment with his bright glassy gray eyes.

Then he added, "He hired me to kill you."

Rufe stared at the well-dressed dude in amazement and snorted, "He did? How the hell you gonna go about that?"

"Like this," Miles said simply, and drawing his gun with unhurried ease he put a bullet between Rufe's wide, startled eyes.

Then Hinton started his horse down the slope through the cedars and rode toward the rocky ridge, calmly replacing the spent cartridge in his gun.

CHAPTER 23

High in the rocks, Bowdry heard the shot that killed Rufe Wadley and he saw Miles Hinton coming unhurriedly up the slope on his sorrel.

But Bowdry had no time to think about Hinton just then, or to wonder what he was up to. For Zeb and Clete were separately crawling through the rocks toward him. He had already spotted them both, only for a moment, but clearly enough for recognition, and from the slight sounds they made he knew roughly where they were now.

Bowdry moved quietly down off the crest of the ridge, using one of the faint trails with which he had become familiar, a trail that zigzagged through the rocks, turning back on itself and seeming to lead nowhere. It took him a good ten minutes to get to a place no more than twenty feet below where he had been before.

He stopped behind a rock and silently watched Zeb crawling with much difficulty up the rough slope, his face red and contorted, sweat glistening in his beard. Panting for breath, Zeb crawled past Bowdry without seeing him, though the latter made no attempt to hide. He slowly turned to watch Zeb go by.

Then Zeb suddenly stopped, blinking sweat from his eyes. He turned his red-bearded face carefully and peered around at the grim, silent gunfighter, who still did not move or speak.

Zeb's gun was in his hand, but he would have to bring it around from an awkward position to fire at Bowdry, who was behind him and over to the left, only his head and shoulders showing above the rock. Zeb knew he would never make it, and after a moment he shrugged and tossed his gun aside.

"All right, Bowdry," he said in a bitter voice. "Looks like you got the edge again. If you promise not to shoot, I'll get the hell out of here, and this time I won't come back."

Bowdry's face got even harder and his blue eyes colder, if that was possible. When he spoke his tone was too quiet and brutal, and when he finished he was already lifting his gun to fire over the rock. "You already had your chance. Just how big a goddamn fool do you take me for?"

He fired two quick shots that sounded almost like one, and Zeb flopped over on his back. Zeb's dirty shirt had got pulled up out of his pants, and his white belly, stained with red, struggled for only a moment before he quit breathing.

A whining bullet tore dust from the rock beside Bowdry. He whirled to see Clete, his green eyes glittering with hatred, bring down his smoking gun to fire again.

Bowdry fired first, a quick snap shot, and Clete was knocked back over the rock behind him. But the pale-haired man held onto his gun, pulled himself up and fired over the rock at Bowdry, who ducked just in time.

A bullet from another gun, in the rocks behind Bowdry, tore through his right shoulder, and he dropped the Russian. Turning as he fell, he sat stunned for a moment with his back to the boulder, blood dripping onto the stock of the dropped pistol. He saw Josh's grinning face up in the rocks, looking down the shiny barrel of a big .45 at him.

In the rocks behind Larkin, and perhaps unknown to him, stood the former desk clerk, Miles Hinton, watching Bowdry with a gleam of interest in his glassy gray eyes, as if wondering what he would do now. Hinton's bone-handled Colt was still in the holster, and it was obvious he meant to just stand back and wait till it was over, then kill whoever was left.

A bitter thought shot through Bowdry's brain. The son of a bitch.

Now when I need the bastard he just stands there. After getting me in all this trouble.

"So long, Bowdry!" Josh called cheerfully. "It's shore been nice knowin' you!"

Bowdry rolled to one side, wincing at a stab of pain in his right shoulder, and Larkin's bullet screamed into the rock near him.

He kept rolling, with bullets whining all around him, until he was in some brush and rocks where he had protection on both sides. Then he drew the New Model Smith & Wesson with his left hand and threw a shot that kicked dust in Josh's face and made him duck from sight.

Bowdry turned his attention to Clete. But Clete was also out of sight, reloading his gun. Both he and Larkin had tried to nail Bowdry as he rolled down the slope.

"Let me get the bastard, Josh!" Anson called to Larkin. "I want him real bad for this hole he put in my side!"

"All right then, he's yores!" Larkin called back. Having failed to finish Bowdry, he sounded a little uneasy. "But if you don't git him, I shore as hell aim to! He's messed around with my girl all he's goin' to!"

While they talked, Bowdry flexed his right hand and tried holding the gun in it. But the whole arm felt numb and stiff and he had trouble moving it. He shook his head and took the gun back in his left hand, a look of worry in his eyes. As a boy he had learned to shoot with either hand, but a gun had always felt more natural in his right hand and that was the hand he had always used when his life was in the balance. After buying a second gun he had either kept it in his waistband with the butt to the right or in a cross-draw holster—in either case to be drawn and fired with his right hand. But now he would have to handle the gun with his left hand, and whether he lived or died depended on how well he handled it.

Still out of sight behind his rock, Clete said maliciously, "I saw you sling that shot with yore left hand, Bowdry. Yore gun hand out of action?"

"Maybe my left hand is my gun hand," Bowdry said.

"Don't you wish?" Anson sneered.

"Better ask your friend up there how close that bullet came," Bowdry suggested.

Hearing him, Larkin called to Anson, "It came damn close! You better be careful, Clete! He ain't outta action yit by a long shot!"

After a moment Anson called back, "If you get a good shot at him, Josh, let the bastard have it!"

Bowdry laughed quietly, and Anson heard him.

"Hell you laughin' at?" the man grunted.

"You shouldn't have come back over here, friend," Bowdry told him. "If you leave this time, somebody will have to carry you. But it won't be Larkin. He won't be able."

"We'll see about that," Anson said. Then he suddenly yelled, "Josh! Did you hear me, Josh?"

"I heard you! But I ain't seen him yit! He's keepin' down behind some rocks and brush!"

"If he moves, let him have it! I'm bleedin' to death, dammit!"

After a moment Larkin asked, "Is there just us two left, Clete?"

"Zeb and Rex is both dead! Bastard killed them! What about Bones and them?"

"They're dead too! Bowdry had a bunch of guns set to go off if anybody stepped on a strang! But Crom went crazy and killed old Bones when Bones tried to take his gun! I think that was a accident, though!"

"Then I guess we're the only ones left! But I saw somebody up there behind you, Josh!"

"Behind me?" Larkin asked in a worried tone. "Where?"

"I don't see him now! I think it was that dude from town, Miles Hinton!"

"What the hell's he doin' around here?" Larkin asked, looking about, from the sound of his voice.

"Fool prob'ly just wants to watch us get killed!" Anson said in a strange, frightened voice. "I guess that's how he has his fun! Rufe already run him off once! If you see him, take a shot at him and maybe he'll get the hell away from here!"

"That's a good idea," Bowdry said. "One thing might interest you though, Josh. He don't just like to watch people get shot. He enjoys using that bone-handled Colt and that shotgun in his blanket roll. All those men everyone thinks I killed—he killed most of them."

"That dude?" Larkin scoffed. "Who you tryin' to kid, Bowdry?"

"That's all right," Bowdry said. "You try taking a shot at him and see what happens."

"You can't fool me with a trick like that," Larkin snorted. "Next you'll be sayin' he's right behind me with a gun."

"He may be for all you know."

"Come on, Bowdry!" Clete cried hoarsely. "Let's get it over with!"

"Be right with you," Bowdry said, watching the rocks where Larkin was. "You ready, Clete? I'm coming after you."

"Come ahead!"

Through the brush Bowdry saw Josh rise up with his gun ready to shoot him in the back when he charged Anson's position. Bowdry lifted the Smith in his left hand and fired, and with a hoarse cry Larkin rose even higher and then fell down the side of a ten-foot rock outcropping, hitting the hard ground below with a thud.

Then Bowdry turned and fired at Clete, who had jumped up behind his rock with a gun in either hand and a wild glitter in his eyes. Anson's green shirt, bloody lower down on the right side, now showed a spot of red higher up, in the exact center of his chest. For just an instant he glared at Bowdry with murderous hatred. Then he fell forward, as rigid as a statue tipped over in a museum, firing both guns at the ground.

Bowdry made sure Clete was dead. Then he went toward Josh over by the rock outcrop, holding the New Model ready in his hand.

Larkin was still alive, and he even managed to sit up as Bowdry came toward him. He looked worriedly at Bowdry's hard face, then glanced at one of his white-handled guns lying nearby. But he did not try to grab the gun. He might die anyway, but he did not want to rush things, and there was still a chance he might talk his way out of this.

Bowdry sat down on a flat rock, favoring his right shoulder, pointing the cocked gun almost casually at Larkin.

Larkin's face got a little red. He looked embarrassed, apologetic, like a boy caught in someone's watermelon patch. Bowdry could have told him it was a bit more serious than that, but the gunfighter remained silent. Nothing he had said lately had done much good. All that talk, he thought, meaning his own talk, when he had warned them to let him alone. Just a waste of time. He had known it would do no good, yet had felt he had to try. Now it was over and there was nothing more to say.

Josh looked down at the bloody front of his shirt. "I reckon I played hell, didn't I?" he said.

Bowdry merely shrugged his good shoulder. The gun in his left hand, still trained on Larkin, did not waver.

"That damn Lucy," Larkin said bitterly. "She got me so I couldn't think straight no more. Playin' her damn silly games. Runnin' over here ever' time we had a few words and lettin' that old man think I meant to kill her or somethin' if I could git my hands on her. And him standin' me off with that shotgun. It was enough to drive anybody crazy. But I never killed him."

"I know that," Bowdry said quietly.

Josh looked at him in surprise. "You do? Then do you know who it was?"

"I think so."

"I know who it was," Larkin said. "It was Lucy!"

Bowdry was silent.

"You don't believe me?" Larkin asked. "I ain't said nothin' till now, but I ain't gonna try to protect her no longer, the way she's been actin' lately. Why you think I even come over here that night? I was lookin' fur her. But when I got here she was already gone and that old man was layin' dead on the floor in a pool of blood. The minute I seen him I knowed she'd killed him. She ain't never said nothin' about it and I don't know for shore what happened. But I got a feelin' that old man told her not to come back no more and she grabbed his gun and shot him. I saw the gun layin' on the floor where she dropped it as she run out the door."

"The gun was pretty close to the old man," Bowdry said. "He could have dropped it when he fell. One cartridge had been fired, but he could have got off a shot at whoever killed him."

"You're kiddin' yoreself, Bowdry," Josh said. "You don't b'lieve she done it 'cause you don't want to b'lieve it!"

"I didn't walk over here to talk about her or the old man," Bowdry said. "I'd already decided you didn't kill him and I was going to let you alone. But you ain't let me alone. You've been trying to get me killed right from the first. Trying to get the Wadleys to do your dirty work for you. When it began to look like they weren't going to get the job done, you tried to help them finish me."

"That's what I been tryin' to tell you!" Larkin exclaimed. "It was on account of her! She had me out of my head with jealousy, so I didn't even half know what I was doin'! It's all that little bitch's fault! But I won't bother you no more. I've learned my lesson this time."

"I've heard that before," Bowdry said, and touched the trigger of the Smith & Wesson. The gun exploded and Josh gave him a startled look of disbelief, then slumped forward.

Bowdry holstered his gun and got to his feet, using his left hand to push himself up. Then holding his right arm with his left hand to ease his throbbing shoulder a little, he made his way slowly through the rocks toward the place where he kept his horse. In passing, his somber glance touched the prone body of Clete. The Wadley men were all dead, Josh was dead, and Bowdry would have a stiff shoulder for a while. Only Miles Hinton, who had caused all the trouble, was still unscratched.

Bowdry stopped in his tracks, the short hair on the back of his neck standing up. It seemed impossible, but he had forgot all about Hinton, had forgot that the killer was skulking around here somewhere, with little doubt waiting to murder anyone who was left alive when the fight was over, even if it was Bowdry. For Hinton would not want to leave Bowdry alive. Bowdry knew or suspected too much about him, and might say the wrong things to the wrong people. And what was one more dead man to someone like Hinton?

Bowdry heard a slight sound behind him and turned, and there Hinton stood with a gun in his hand and a wolfish grin on his face that gave the lie to his nice clothes and polished manners.

"I don't guess I need you anymore, Bowdry," Hinton said in a conversational tone. "But I'm obliged for all you've done. You came in real handy."

He cocked the blue-steel Colt and started to squeeze the trigger. But at that instant a rifle crashed from the rocks above them and Hinton went rigid, an odd look on his face as he gazed past Bowdry up the rough slope. A moment later he pitched forward on his face, firing his pistol at the ground.

Bowdry turned his head and saw Lucy Reardon standing in the rocks with a Winchester, which she slowly lowered.

Bowdry, his shoulder bandaged and his arm in a sling, led the dark chestnut down to the waterhole, and then on to the old shack, having saddled the horse with some difficulty. The strawberry roan stood ground-reined near the corral, and Lucy, handling a shovel like a man, was working on a fresh grave beside the old man's.

Bowdry sat down in the shack doorway and watched in bleak silence until she finished putting rocks on top of the grave and came over with the shovel.

"You don't mind, do you?" she asked. "About me burying him there?"

Bowdry shrugged his good shoulder. "Why should I mind?"

"That's right," she said. "I keep forgetting. The old man wasn't anything to you."

She turned and looked toward the graves, the shovel still over her shoulder. "It seems fitting in a way. Him buried beside the man he killed."

Bowdry glanced up at her. "He said you killed the old man."

She looked at him in amazement, her mouth open before she spoke. "He said *I* killed him!"

Bowdry nodded, smiling faintly.

Her face reddened behind the freckles and she frowned at Larkin's grave. "Why, that low-down lying son of a—why would he say a crazy thing like that?"

Bowdry again moved his left shoulder. "I think he believed you really did kill the old man. Just like you think it was him."

"Wasn't it him?"

"I don't think so," Bowdry said.

She watched him a moment, then suddenly exclaimed, "*You* don't think it was me, do you?"

He shook his head. "I never really thought it was you. I think you could have done it. But you would have left some sign, and there wasn't any. That made me pretty sure it wasn't you, and when you kept after me about his horse, that convinced me. If you killed him, you wouldn't want the horse around to remind you."

Lucy swallowed and looked silently toward the graves, her eyes damp. Then she gave Bowdry a puzzled look. "If it wasn't Josh or any of the Wadleys, who was it?"

"The man you shot up there in those rocks," Bowdry told her.

"*Him*! Why on earth would he kill the old man?"

Bowdry shrugged. "Why would he kill any of the men he's killed? Why would he try to kill me? Maybe he just liked to kill. But my guess is he killed the old man to get this trouble started. He knew everyone would think it was the Wadleys, and then, if he was careful he could kill all of them he wanted to and everyone would think it was me doing it."

"But why would he want to kill them? He must have had some reason."

"I figure someone hired him."

"Harris Thacker?"

Bowdry nodded. "That's my guess."

"It's all just a guess though, isn't it? You're not even sure it was him killed Mr. Pollard."

"He's the only one I know of who could have done it without leaving any sign. That man was mighty good at covering his tracks. If it wasn't him, then it had to be Larkin—and he had to be the most convincing liar I've ever come up against."

"He was that, all right," Lucy said, glancing toward the graves. "He could make me believe things I knew weren't true, and I hate to think what all he's got you believing about me."

"It don't really matter," Bowdry said, getting to his feet. "It's high time I got the hell out of here."

"You and me both," Lucy Reardon said. "I should have cleared out a long time ago, but I couldn't get Josh to go with me. Now I'm going by myself." She looked at Bowdry. "Unless you'd like some company. I could cook and keep an eye on that shoulder for a while."

Bowdry shrugged. "Suit yourself. But if you wake up some morning and find me gone, don't say I didn't warn you."

Lucy Reardon smiled. "That's what Josh told me, and he left a lot. But he always came back, and if I tried to leave he always came after me."

"I'm not Josh."

"I know. That worries me a little."

Riding out of the country, they were glimpsed here and there in the distance, a tall man on a fine dark chestnut and a red-haired woman on a strawberry roan. But then they vanished into the desert and after that no one ever reported seeing them again. How long they remained together or what became of them, no one knows.

Half-forgotten memories of men now dead, an old gun with traces of blood on the walnut stock, found in the rocks above the Pollard shack. Not much else remains after all this time.

Thank you for reading
The Man Called Bowdry
by Van Holt.

If you enjoyed this story, please leave a review about
your experience on Amazon.

More hellbound gunslinging westerns by Van Holt:

Blood in the Hills
http://amzn.to/16jWNvB

Curly Bill and Ringo
http://amzn.to/Z6AhSH

Dead Man's Trail
http://amzn.to/ZcPJ47

Death in Black Holsters
http://amzn.to/1aHxGcv

Dynamite Riders
http://amzn.to/ZyhHmg

Hellbound Express
http://amzn.to/11i3NcY

Hunt the Killers Down
http://amzn.to/Z7UHjD

Riding for Revenge
http://amzn.to/13gLILz

Rubeck's Raiders
http://amzn.to/14CDxwU

Shiloh Stark
http://amzn.to/12ZJxcV

Shoot to Kill
http://amzn.to/18zA1qm

Six-Gun Solution
http://amzn.to/10t3H3N

Six-Gun Serenade
Coming Soon!

So Long, Stranger
http://amzn.to/16c0I2J

Son of a Gunfighter
Coming Soon!

The Antrim Guns
Coming Soon!

The Bounty Hunters
http://amzn.to/10gJQ6C

The Bushwhackers
http://amzn.to/13ln4JO

The Fortune Hunters
http://amzn.to/11i3VsO

The Last of the Fighting Farrells
http://amzn.to/Z6AyVI

The Long Trail
http://amzn.to/137P9c8ß

The Stranger From Hell
http://amzn to/12qVVqd

The Vultures
http://amzn.to/12bjeGl

Wild Country
http://amzn.to/147xUDq

Wild Desert Rose
http://amzn.to/XH7Y27